BRODY'S BRIDE

SEVEN BRIDES FOR SEVEN BROTHERS
BOOK ONE

KATHLEEN LAWLESS

ISBN ebook: 978-0-9937701-7-3

ISBN print: 978-1-989873-49-6

Seven Brides for Seven Brothers Reviews

What reviewers are saying about the *Seven Brides for Seven Brothers* series...

"GREAT SERIES!!!" Top 500 reviewer

"If you have not picked up the series, do yourself a favor, you will be glad you do."

"I loved the continuity in the series—and the resolution"

"Sweet and romantic."

"This entire series is going into my library to be read again and again."

"I just love reading Kathleen's books—they keep me coming back for more."

If you haven't already done so, sign up for my VIP Reader's Newsletter and be the first to hear about free books, fan-priced sales, and my new series. Details at the end of the book.

Dedication

Dedicated to my real-life hero, John Steel
Who brings me coffee in bed every morning when I
wake up.

CHAPTER 1

Laura's heart raced nearly as fast as the stage coach traveling the road from Yuma to Bullet. She couldn't believe she was back in Arizona after ten long years. Let alone in collusion with Brody's sworn enemy.

She wondered how long until her path crossed with Brody's.

"Not long till we reach Bullet, lovely Laura."

She glanced at her companion, masking her disdain. Little Guy, as she thought of him, rather than by his given name of Jeffrey, had no idea how useful Laura was finding him.

"I'm sure I'll find it every bit as charming as you said, Jeffrey. And imagine a small town being prosperous enough to build a school." There had been no school there ten years ago.

"It was Pa's idea. Can't have hooligans running around the countryside with no education." Little Guy smirked. "Wait till he finds out I brought back a bona-fide school teacher from Los Angeles."

Laura cast her eyes demurely downward. "I hope he

doesn't find it too presumptuous of me to simply arrive unannounced."

"Leave me to handle Pa." She could almost see Jeffrey's chest puff with importance.

"And who, pray tell, is your sire, young man?" asked their coach mate, obviously a foreigner, judging by the man's clipped accent and city clothing.

While Jeffrey droned on with glowing attributes to his father, which Laura had already suffered through, she turned her attention to the passing scenery. Arizona's countryside had barely changed in the years since she had snuck over here from Yuma to see Brody.

Would he even remember her?

Being back still seemed surreal. All because of a random conversation overheard.

Standing in line at the postal station, her ears had perked up when Jeffrey mentioned the town of Bullet and boasted to a companion about his father's exploits there. According to Jeffrey, nothing could stop Hawkes Sr. from taking over every lock, stock, and barrel, including a certain ranch owned by a bunch of rag-tag losers who called themselves brothers.

Brody's ranch.

Her heart twisted with sadness recalling the last time she had set eyes on Brody. Did he still hate her for what she had done?

Determinedly, she had swallowed her distaste for Jeffrey Hawkes and arranged a chance meeting, the first of several. Eventually, she let him 'talk her into' going to Bullet with him to teach in the town's new schoolhouse. She deserved an award for her acting ability as she pretended to be grateful to him for taking her under his wing. She knew, in order to pull this off, to spy on Jeffrey's father for Brody, it had to seem like it was all Jeffrey's idea she was here.

Her hair, pale gold originally, had darkened over the years to a rich burnished chestnut color kissed by the California sun and shot through with lighter strands. She wore spectacles, not that she needed them, but she believed it made her look more like a schoolmarm; older than her twenty-eight years.

When they arrived in Bullet and alighted from the coach, she glanced up and down the dust-trodden Main Street, as if seeing it for the first time. "Why Jeffrey, I don't see a single hotel or rooming house anywhere."

"There is a rooming house next street over, but it's too rough for a lady such as yourself. You'll stay at the Ranch with Pa and I."

"Oh, I don't think that would be seemly at all. What might people think?" she said demurely, secretly applauding the chance to get close to Hawkes Sr. Close enough to learn what his evil plans entailed.

"Don't you worry about what people think. My Pa takes care of all that."

SEATED in the comfy old ranch house kitchen of the Copper Moon Ranch, Brody Mason looked up as his surrogate brother, Braydon, pulled up a chair.

"Got us some new intel on Hawkes," Braydon said.

Anytime one of them mentioned Hawkes's name, the other six paid attention. The twins overheard Braydon and joined them first. All the Masons hated the man with good reason, but the Brody and the twins had an especially keen interest in seeing Hawkes thoroughly and irrevocably destroyed.

"Out with it," Bishop said.

"Waiting on the others," Braydon said.

One by one the other three ambled in and found seats around the massive scrubbed pine table Brody had made in his youth. Not only did the table dominate the kitchen, it doubled as a work bench, learning desk, or operating table, depending on what the brothers needed it for on any given day.

Brody watched the way Braydon grinned at each brother in turn. The man surely did love an audience.

"Seems Hawkes has hired a right comely school teacher for his new schoolhouse, and he fancies her," Braydon said.

"Don't see what that's got to do with us," dark and brooding Bradley said, picking at a sliver in his thumb.

"Remember, piece by piece, no matter how long it takes, we're taking the man down," Braydon said.

The others nodded in agreement and Brody felt a wave of gratitude and admiration for the unorthodox family he helped create here at the Copper Moon. These men were his brothers in the soul. He'd trust them with his life.

"Anything and everything Hawkes owns, or covets, slowly gets taken over by us," Braydon continued. "He sets his sights on the little schoolmarm, one of us needs to woo her away."

"My vote's with you," one of the others said. "You're the ladies' man hereabouts."

"Just because I'm better acquainted with soap and water than you are—"

Brody stepped between the two men before moods escalated. "Settle down you two. The only fair way to decide who woos the fair school teacher's favor is to draw straws."

There was a shuffling of feet and a few murmurs of dissent. Brody held up his hand. "We're in this together, or did you all forget that little detail?"

"Anyone seen her?" Benjamin asked.

"Haven't got a look at her yet. But she must be something if Hawkes is gunning for another trophy," Braydon said.

They all fell silent. As if any of them needed a reminder of what Hawkes had done to one of their own. And the trophy he flaunted from that killing.

"Fair enough." Bishop set to work fetching the straws.

One by one, each of them drew. Brody went last and his heart fell when the short straw was revealed. He narrowed his gaze on Bishop. "You rig this?" Bishop and his twin were professional con artists. He wouldn't put anything past them.

"I swear," Bishop said. "Fair draw."

Brody stared down at the straw in his hand. Wooing a stranger. He hadn't got close to any females in that way since Laura.... He tamped down the thought. Closed book. Ancient history.

"Looks like I have to do everything around here," he grumbled.

It wasn't long before Brody learned the lady in question had taken up residence at the Hawkes spread. Given the history between him and Hawkes, he could hardly go riding up to the front door, hat in hand. He'd have to come up with an excuse to seek out the lady at Bullet's new school.

THE HAWKES RANCH house echoed emptily as Laura made her way downstairs. She'd never been in a house so devoid of life. If the pervading air of gloom was anything to go by, this house had never known happier days.

The furniture in the great hall was dark and heavy, like something from Medieval times. The dining room table would easily sit more than a dozen guests. The parlor next to it was huge, the shroud-like drapes drawn against the sunlight. She poked her head into the den across the hall, next to the kitchen, and wrinkled her nose in distaste at the stale smell of cigar smoke.

Hawkes Sr. had purportedly been away on a mysterious business errand when she and Jeffrey arrived and Laura was going crazy with boredom. Since no one was around to stop her, Laura traveled the great hall's length to the far end and opened the French doors that led to the back of the house. A flagstone pathway meandered through a variety of plants that were obviously lovingly maintained by Hawkes's down-trodden-looking work crew of Mexicans.

Other than the occasional curious glance, she might as well have been invisible.

The pathway led to a large open pond with a fountain in the center spraying a high arc of water. The droplets caught the sun as they fell, creating a rainbow prism effect. Hawkes must have spent a fortune bringing water from the river to maintain the grounds and the keep the pond flowing.

A few unfamiliar water plants dotted the surface of the otherwise calm water. If she leaned over, she could see her reflection near the edge.

"Don't get too close."

She whirled to see Jeffrey behind her. "Mercy. You gave me a start." How had she not heard him approach?

"It's deeper than it looks."

"It certainly must have been an undertaking, having this built."

"Father has many grand ideas."

Laura would just bet that he did.

"My mother drowned here last year," Jeffrey said, his brow furrowed as he stared into the watery depths. "I was the one who found her."

"I'm so sorry," Laura said. "That must have been terrible for you."

"You know how it feels to lose a parent," Jeffrey said. "I felt that when we originally met. You understand in the way others can't."

"Do tell me again how that meeting came about," said a deep voice behind her.

She didn't imagine the way Jeffrey tensed when confronted by a burly man whom Laura assumed to be Hawkes. She studied him silently. She had expected someone dressed to the nines in the role of the estate owner, rather than this shabby, dirt-covered bully.

"Father, this is the school-teacher I told you about in my telegram. Miss Laura Kismet."

"Sorry I wasn't cleaned up and here to greet you," Hawkes said. "As you can see, I'm a hands-on kind of man, unlike my son."

Something in the way he looked at her as he spoke made Laura feel he'd happily have his hands on her. Suddenly she needed a bath.

"Jeffrey assured me my being here would not be an imposition," she said.

Hawkes's lips curled in what might have passed for a smile, except it didn't touch his mean, narrow eyes. "Anything but, Miss Kismet. Anything but."

He turned away, pausing only to add over his shoulder. "Your contract is ready to be signed. I'll see you in my den before supper."

WITHIN DAYS, four of the brothers packed up and headed west with a herd of cattle to sell. The ranch always felt quiet when any of the others were away, which didn't help soothe Brody's worries till everyone landed back safe. He knew, much as him and his were quietly out for Hawkes, Hawkes was gunning for them in equal measure.

Brody straightened to see Bishop riding up to where he was surveying the latest round of what the sheriff dismissed as 'mischief'. Brody and his brothers knew it was more than mischief. A deliberate rerouting of the irrigation canals and estuaries from the Colorado River left the cattle with no water out here in the back pastures of the ranch. Brody straightened, took off his Stetson, and swiped at his forehead with one forearm.

"Thought maybe you could use a hand," Bishop said, as he swung out of the saddle.

"I don't like leaving the ranch unattended with the others away."

"Blake's there. He sent me to check on you. We all know..." Bishop gave him a dark look. "Alone out here... Anything could happen."

Anything being Hawkes.

Brody wouldn't put a thing past the man when it came to getting what he wanted. Right now, he wanted the Copper Moon. Had done for as long as Brody could remember, going back to the days when his uncle was still alive. He figured there was more than one reason Hawkes was set on owning the ranch so bad. And if the others got wind of the lollapalooza of a secret he was keeping, his uncle's deathbed disclosure....

Brody plopped his Stetson back on his head. His life had pretty much been built around secrets. Nothing new there.

"More of Hawkes's handiwork?" Bishop asked.

"His instigation. I'm betting he's not so quick to get his hands dirty these days."

They both fell silent, remembering that one life-altering night when Hawkes was only too happy to get his hands bloody. They had been too late to stop Hawkes from killing the twins' older brother, but Brody's vendetta toward Hawkes went back further than that.

The full moon that night had borne witness to the brothers' vow to destroy Hawkes. An oath the seven of them had sworn in blood.

"Leave it till tomorrow," Bishop said. "We'll all come out and help."

Brody nodded. He'd managed to divert enough water back into the canal so the cattle could water. They had a chunk of capital invested in this herd and it would be some time before they were ready to be driven out west to sell.

Brody mounted up and his horse fell into step behind Bishop's, which surprised him. Usually Phoenix insisted on taking the lead.

Brody and Bishop arrived at the Copper Moon ranch house just in time to see the sheriff and Hawkes dismounting out front. Brody kept his face impassible. It was that time again. Time when the sheriff came snooping around on 'official business', determining cash value of county properties before delivering an assessment to the Board of Equalization, from which the owner's tax bill for the year was determined.

Brody would love to order them off the land, and hated that he couldn't. Every year Sheriff Yates officially hired Hawkes as his 'assistant' to help assess the local properties.

Hawkes took full advantage of the power his temporary role afforded him.

"Hear tell you've done some improvements to the place," the sheriff said.

"Nothing new since year before last," Brody said.

"Hawkes stopped by a while back. Said you've got some new outbuildings. Isn't that so, Guy?"

Brody longed to wipe the smirk off Hawkes's face. Wouldn't the man relish any excuse to snoop around the ranch? And inevitably showed up when Brody and the others weren't around. Even today, Hawkes was covered in more dirt than one would expect from doing property assessments. Which told Brody he'd been someplace he had no business going.

As if he'd sensed trouble, Blake, one of the brothers, appeared from the direction of the barn, wiping his hands on a greasy rag. Brody gave an imperceptible nod. There was strength in numbers.

To his visitors, Brody waved an expansive hand. "Nothing new, as you can see."

It was a game they played up every year. All across the county, Sheriff and Hawkes deliberately inflated everyone's land value. If the owner couldn't pay the exorbitant taxes, the land was then confiscated and sold in a public sale to, guess who? Guy Hawkes.

It was a dirty little deal that had been going on as long as Brody could remember. He wondered if Hawkes had any clue why, these last few years, land owners hereabouts had all managed to pay their taxes, effectively thwarting his greedy land grab.

Sheriff Yates hitched his trousers over his sagging belly and spat a plug of tobacco on the ground near Brody's feet.

"Be a real shame if some of your boys didn't make it back from California before taxes are due."

Brody narrowed his gaze on the crooked lawman. "Don't see it being a problem."

"Anything can happen out on the trail." Coming from Hawkes, the words sounded more of a threat than a voice of concern.

Brody laid a light hand on Bishop's arm, knowing exactly where the other man's gaze was honed. Hawkes wore the handmade knife on his belt as a trophy, one he'd taken from the twins' older brother right before he hung his lifeless body from a dead tree.

Brody and the others never lost sight of their pledge that night, to piece by piece destroy Hawkes and everything he held near and dear.

"You done here?" Blake asked.

"For now," Sheriff Yates said. The two men mounted up, but took their time leaving.

"Good riddance," Brody said under his breath as the men rode away, their mounts' hooves kicking up a fine cloud of dust behind them.

Blake spoke up. "Think Hawkes and the sheriff know what you're about? How suddenly everyone around here manages to get their taxes paid on time?"

"Not much they can do, even if they do suspect."

They both knew it wasn't true. There was lots Hawkes could do to sabotage the ranch and make their lives miserable. And as he'd proved before, he wasn't above killing anyone in his way.

Bishop spoke up. "I'll feel a damn sight better once the others are back."

A week passed during which Brody never left the ranch, using a multitude of excuses to himself to stick close. Never far from mind was the ridiculous task he'd been set. What did he know about wooing a woman? What if he made a fool of himself and she laughed in his face? Nothing more Brody hated than being made a laughing stock.

Unsuccessfully he tried to stop his mind from going down that dark pathway to the last time he saw Laura.

Or the first.

He'd known right from the get-go that she was above his station, but his ego got the better of him. Made sure she was intrigued by his eighteen-year-old swagger and confidence.

Up until that day, anytime his thoughts strayed toward the fairer sex he pulled to mind his ma running off and leaving him, choosing her fancy snake oil salesman over him. He had thought he was past it when he met Laura. Everything about her made him feel good.

Much as he tried to deny it, those magical times with Laura had never completely faded from that special place she'd carved in his heart. Even though a part of him had died the day she out-and-out rejected him in front of what felt like the entire town of Yuma, he couldn't manage to forget her. Her touch. Her scent. Her taste.

He heaved a sigh. Maybe this little challenge facing him, to woo the schoolmarm, would shake off those cobwebbed memories once and for all.

He'd heard the others wagering a bet among themselves as to when he would finally get gussied up and head for the schoolhouse. Trouble was, he couldn't show up all random-like, he needed a reason. Then it came to him. Blake would kill him when he found out, but by then it would be too late.

Brody took his time getting ready. Shaved, slicked down his hair, put on his best shirt and polished his boots. Without a word to anyone he saddled up Phoenix and made his way to Bullet.

The schoolhouse stood off to one side, next to a field where the kids could run around and play, shiny as a new pin. Bullet, like all this part of Arizona soon as you moved away from the river, was a dustbowl, dry to the bone. Temperatures ranged from hot to hellish hot.

He tilted back his head and studied the exterior of the building. It looked nicer than the one in Yuma. Cleaner too. Red brick must have cost Hawkes a fortune, but the man surely did like to flaunt his wealth.

Slowly Brody dismounted and tied Phoenix to the hitching post out front. Feeling like he was facing his executioner, he made his way up two steps to the front door, only to find it locked tight.

His heart lightened, feeling a reprieve. His steps were lighter, too, as he made his way back to his horse. He'd barely touched the reins, when he heard a female voice behind him.

"Brody. Brody is that you?"

Slowly he turned. Laura stood before him like a vision from the past, one he wasn't sure was real or imagined. All the pain and confusion from ten years ago rushed through him, filling his head with so much chatter he couldn't hear a thing.

CHAPTER 2

Brody waited for the rushing in his ears to subside. He blinked several times, but Laura remained solidly in front of him. Next to her was a smart-looking carriage, one he recognized as belonging to Hawkes, and his gut tightened.

Sunlight glinted on the strands of hair that had escaped her bonnet; hair a few shades darker than he recalled. Something else was different as well; spectacles perched on the bridge of her nose, which was scattered with a dusting of freckles.

He wondered if she still hated those freckles he had once found so adorable.

He cleared his throat, hoping his voice didn't let him down like his traitorous heart. "I was looking for the new schoolmarm."

"Congratulations. You found her." Her delicate feet stirred clouds of dust as she moved past him up the steps and pulled out a key. "Come in."

"You're the one working for Hawkes?" He couldn't have

been more stunned if she'd pulled out a knife and stuck it in his gut.

He saw her back stiffen ever so slightly. "A girl has to make a living."

"And staying on his ranch." He couldn't prevent the accusing tone underlying his words. Maybe she didn't know him and Hawkes were mortal enemies.

Graceful as ever, she moved to the front of the sparkly new classroom which smelled of fresh-cut lumber. She removed her bonnet and hung it on a peg near her desk before she turned to face him. He hadn't moved far from the doorway.

"No one knows I once lived in Arizona, Brody, and I'd like to keep it that way. Leave the past where it belongs."

By no one, she meant Hawkes.

He forced his uncooperative tongue to move. "Never expected to see you back in these parts."

"Life deals us unexpected hands." He flinched beneath her disapproving look. "You of all people should appreciate that."

She'd always disapproved of him gambling, and her words drove the point home.

"Hawkes is still a no-good son-of-a-bitch."

"You're speaking about my employer." Her words were as stiff as her ramrod straight back, but he saw the way she rolled a piece of chalk between her fingers and the sight of it gave him pause. Maybe she wasn't indifferent to him after all. His mission was to woo her, not antagonize her; even if that was before he knew the new school teacher was Laura.

He narrowed his gaze. Maybe if he won her over and dumped her on her cute little behind, they'd be even. Maybe she'd disappear from his dreams forever.

"Now what can I do for you?" she asked.

He forced himself to move through the new classroom toward where she stood near the desk. "This is a tad awkward," he said. "I didn't know you were the new school teacher when I showed up here."

"I don't see what difference that makes."

That was because she knew nothing about the conversation between him and his brothers. A plan that had looked so workable a week ago, steal the lady's affections from Hawkes, had hit a major hurdle right out of the gate.

Or perhaps not. Getting her out to the ranch to tutor Blake might rile Hawkes enough that he'd send her packing.

Brody dug deep to try and find that buried charm he had used to woo her ten years earlier. "You look good, Laura."

He noticed her eyes didn't quite meet his, so clearly she was not as indifferent to him as she pretended. "A lot of years have gone by, Brody. Now out with it. I know stall tactics when I see them."

She always did see through him like a window.

He hung his head a little, as if to admit she'd caught him out, then glanced at her from beneath the brim of his hat. "Blake will kill me when he finds out. But I was hoping to hire the new teacher to help him learn to read. It has to be secret-like. The others don't know he can't read and he's real sensitive about it."

"Why can't you teach him to read?"

Damn, this wasn't going to be easy. "Well, I tried a few different times over the years, but the letters don't make any more sense to him than the words. It's like it's all backwards gibberish. Kind of funny though. When it comes to engines and mechanical stuff that boy can just look at it and figure out how it works. Can take it apart and put it back together in his sleep. He's not stupid."

Laura nodded and moved to stand behind her desk as if to put a physical barrier between them. "It sounds like a disorder called word blind. Not much is known, from the little I've read about it, but people afflicted see letters and numbers backwards."

"So he can't be taught to read." Which didn't much matter. Blake had been his excuse for seeking out the teacher.

Now that he knew the teacher was Laura, he didn't know what to do. Except get the hell away before he said or did something stupid. Like forgave her for breaking his heart, for rejecting and humiliating him in front of the whole world.

"Anything is possible, but it would take someone with far greater skills than I possess."

Brody rocked back and forth from his heels to his toes. This little ruse of his had been a stupid idea from the start, made even worse by the fact the new teacher was Laura.

He should leave Laura to deal with Hawkes. But he couldn't.

Hawkes destroyed everything in his path. He couldn't let the man destroy Laura. He had to get her out of there.

His head demanded he leave.

His heart propelled him to her side.

"Tell me straight. Why'd you come back here?" He clenched his fists at his sides to keep from reaching out, from taking her in his arms.

"It's not what you think, Brody." Again, that look of hers, peeling back his skin, looking straight inside him. His heart beat faster. His chest felt tight.

Once upon a time he thought he knew every damn thing about her. Now he had no idea if he ever had. His gut clenched. He wouldn't be making that mistake again. "You have no idea what I think."

With that, he turned on his heel and marched from the classroom.

Her softly-spoken words followed him. "I did once."

With Brody gone, Laura let out a shaky breath and lowered herself into the chair behind her desk. Her legs were so weak she doubted she could have stood another second.

She had known it was inevitable that her path would cross with Brody's, but hadn't counted on it being so soon. Had thought she'd have more time to settle in to life in Bullet. To get established.

She also hadn't counted on the depth of feelings she still had for Brody. Standing alongside him, the intervening ten years had melted away as if they never existed. She longed to touch him, to kiss away the hurt and disappointment in his eyes. Hurt and pain caused by her.

If she hadn't physically stepped behind her desk, she'd have been tempted to fling herself in his arms and plead with him to forgive her. To let him know she came back because of him. But she could never let him find that out.

Foolhardy. That's what returning to Bullet had been. Ridiculous to think she could get the goods on what Hawkes was scheming in his vendetta against Brody.

Brody was a grown man, more than capable of seeing to his own interests and well-being. Once before, she had done what she thought best for him and had succeeded only in alienating him forever. How much worse could she make things?

Could he despise her more than he already did?

With school not set to open for a week, she planned on using some of that time to ready the classroom. Brightly colored pictures of the alphabet and numbers were only the first step in making it a place to learn and have fun at the same time.

And she needed to find a place to live. She had no intention of staying out on Hawkes's ranch a minute longer than she had to. Hawkes Sr. was a bully and a tyrant and just the way he looked at her made her skin crawl. Little Guy was a wimp she could easily control and manipulate, but the father was another animal all together.

She hadn't known the Hawkes family when she was growing up in Yuma, and the only time she had come to Bullet to see Brody, nothing and no one else existed in her teenage world. She choked down a deprecating laugh. Had she ever truly been that young and naïve?

Apparently, she had.

She had thought that by denouncing Brody in front of the entire town in Yuma, she could somehow protect him and make things right. Nothing in her life had gone right since.

She locked the school and took a little stroll around Bullet's main streets. What she had hoped to see, a tidy sign stating 'room for rent' didn't materialize. She was just about ready to give up and head back to the Hawkes spread when she heard the clean, clear sound of music coming through an open window.

She stopped to listen to the pianist playing the familiar notes of *Clementine*. When it was over, she clapped her hands together in appreciation.

The window opened further and a ginger-haired girl stuck her head out. "I didn't know I had an audience."

"Sorry. I didn't mean to intrude. It was just the friendliest sound I've heard since I arrived."

"Wait there a sec."

She barely had time to turn around before the redhead was at her side with a friendly smile.

"That doesn't say much for Bullet. I'm Amanda Cooke, by the way." She extended a freckled hand toward Laura.

"Laura Kismet," she said. "Nice to meet you."

Amanda cocked her head to one side like an inquiring robin. "What brings you to Bullet?"

"I'm the newly-hired school teacher."

The other woman's smile faded. She pulled her hand away. "Staying out at the Hawkes place." It was a statement rather than a question.

Laura made a face. She had forgotten how quickly news spread in a small town. "Only temporarily until I find someplace closer to the school."

"Which of the Hawkes men have you set your sights on? Senior controls the purse strings."

"Neither." Laura repressed a shudder at the thought. "Jeffrey was kind enough to offer me the job and help me get settled is all."

"Jeffrey's not supposed to think for himself. I hear he caught grief bringing you to town without clearing it with his daddy first."

"Then you understand I can't stay there any longer. I was hoping to find someone in town who has a room to rent."

"There's rooms over the saloon but you wouldn't want to stay there." Amanda's friendly smile returned, as if she'd forgiven Laura for staying at the Hawkes's ranch. "Could be worse than the Hawkes place." She wrinkled her nose as if in thought. "I know. Why don't you stay here? Ma's away so there's lots of room."

Laura hesitated. She hated being so suspicious by nature. But who opened their house to a total stranger on first acquaintance?

"I mean, you're a school teacher. You gotta be a good person, right?"

Laura wished her world was still so simple. "What if we don't get along?"

Amanda shrugged. "I get along with most folks. Easier that way."

"I'll pay you a fair rent," Laura said.

"Course you will," said Amanda. "I'll get the room ready. You can move your things in tomorrow."

"Can I ask you something?"

"Sure can," Amanda said.

"Will folks in town send their children to school next week?"

"Why do you ask?"

"Hawkes owns the school. Doesn't strike me he's well-liked from what I can see."

"Like doesn't enter into it. Folks around here do what he says. Bad luck has a way of following anyone who doesn't."

"I met a man earlier. Name of Mason. Lives on a spread west of town."

Inexplicably Amanda turned bright red in the face. "Name of Mason? Which one of them did you meet?"

Laura deliberately didn't answer too quickly. "I think he said his name was Brody."

Amanda's color receded. "Brody's the oldest. There's seven of them living out at the Copper Moon. See a few of them in town once in a while. They keep pretty much to themselves."

Laura nodded, as if to say that's what she'd thought. But she did wonder at the sudden bloom of color to Amanda's cheeks. She'd have to find out what that was all about.

Laura returned to her borrowed horse and buggy feeling considerably lighter of heart. She not only had somewhere to live, she also might have a new friend, which would help make life in Bullet more palatable. Even though she wouldn't be living under Hawkes's roof, she had to maintain contact with the two men; professionally as regards to the school, and personally as to finding out plans to sabotage the Copper Moon and its residents.

All without Brody learning why she really came back to Arizona.

That last part shouldn't be too hard. It didn't sound like he had a child he'd be sending her way for educating. Her heart lurched with a sad hiccup at the thought of Brody with a wife, a family; something she hadn't even considered. She gave the reins a gentle slap. Ten years had passed. Anything was possible. She and Brody were no longer smitten teens.

A QUIET WEEK passed on the Copper Moon. A week during which, no matter how hard he worked, Brody's brain teased him constantly, replaying his meeting with Laura at the school house. If possible, she'd grown more lovely over the years; matured from a girl to a woman. A woman his heart had never forgotten, any more than he had forgotten her scent. Her touch. Her taste.

Brody, Blake and Bishop were just finishing the evening meal when they heard the sound of approaching horses.

Brody rose first. "Sounds like the rest of them are back, right on time."

He and the others herded to the front porch where the incoming riders pulled up in front of the house instead of heading for the barn, the first sign that something was wrong. Brody did a quick headcount. All accounted for.

Bradley, his arm in a makeshift sling, was the last one to dismount.

"What the blazes—?" Brody spoke first.

Barron, a mirror image of his twin brother Bishop, spoke for the group. "They were waiting for us when we crossed the border."

"Who was waiting?"

Barron shrugged. "You know that canyon on the far side of the river?"

Brody nodded grimly.

Braydon spoke up. "It was no ordinary ambush. They got us from all sides and surrounded us. Winged Bradley with a warning shot, but I don't think they meant to shoot anybody. Clear they were after the money."

Brody felt his innards sink down around his knees. It was more than money, it was the power money bought. The power he needed to take from Hawkes. "Recognize any of them?"

Braydon shook his head. "They wore masks. Covered up the brands on the horses, but have to say, sure looked like they could have come from Hawkes's place."

"Put money on it." Benjamin spoke up for the first time since arriving.

"Well, you're all back in one piece, that's the main thing," Brody said gruffly. "See to the horses and get a hot meal into yourselves. And from now on, nobody goes anyplace alone. Not even on the ranch."

"Brody!" There was a chorus of protests from all sides.

Brody got it. With the exception of the twins, all of them were loners; having kicked around on their own for quite some time before finding their way to the ranch and joining the brotherhood he had created.

The men were all very different. Each had his own story,

his own past, his own secrets. But one thing they all had in common, two things really.... They were loyal to the death. And they each had a personal reason to help destroy Hawkes.

Brody helped Bradley inside the ranch house where Bishop got out the first aid kit. The kit saw a fair bit of use, and Brody knew Bishop had a lot of practice honing his skills long before they met up.

Bishop's twin had a gift with his fists. The two set up boxing matches and collected the bets. Barron would either win or throw the fight depending on who was the favorite. Bishop had patched his brother up many a time over the years.

Bradley eyed the kit warily. "Get that stuff away from me. It stinks and it smarts."

"You'll feel more than a sting if the wound gets infected," Brody said mildly.

Bradley continued to eye the contents of the first aid kit suspiciously. Finally, he rose. "I'd better get me a good strong drink first."

Braydon spoke up. "Bring the bottle. I think we could all use a drink."

With practiced moves Bishop cleaned, stitched, and dressed Bradley's wound. Bradley went white, bit his lip, but kept quiet during the procedure, after which Brody rewarded him with a bowl of stew and a companionable pat on his good shoulder.

"Count yourself lucky it wasn't worse."

Bradley grunted.

Brody stood off to one side, watching, as the others ate and drank amidst much good-natured bickering. They were a good group. Better than kin. Tomorrow he'd have no choice but head into Yuma and hit the gambling halls. It was a curse and a blessing, the skill he'd inherited from his old man with cards and numbers.

The number part came in handy doing the accounts and bills for the ranch. The gambling part was necessary from time to time even though he wished it wasn't. They had a month until the taxes were due, but they'd need more than tax money. They had to buy more livestock to fatten up and drive west. And there was always the matter of some of his neighbors coming up short on their own tax bills. Everybody hereabouts counted on him. Some days he wished it wasn't so.

Brody was up before the others, in the barn saddling Phoenix, when Braydon found him. "Weren't thinking about breaking your own house rule and going off alone were you?"

"Your time is better spent here. Nothing to be helped by you trailing off to Yuma with me."

"They didn't get all the cash, you know."

"Glad to hear it." Brody tightened the cinch.

"Figured you might need some start-up capital." Braydon pulled a roll of bills from his pocket.

"I got enough to get started. Hang onto that."

"Suit yourself," Braydon said. "But I'm coming with you."

Braydon was as stubborn as he was charming and agreeable at turns. He was also a good wingman.

"Stick close, then. No hightailing it off to see your fancy ladies."

Braydon just grinned as he saddled up.

Brody gave him a look. "I know that smile."

Every one of the men appreciated Braydon sharing his knowledge of the fairer sex, gleaned from growing up as he had at Madam Zara's. Braydon never had learned which one of the working girls was his mother, but they all spoiled and cossetted him and made sure he had an education in every sense of the word, from books and music to the birds and the bees. Braydon had enjoyed the most affluent, if the least traditional, upbringing of any of the others, and appreciated the finer things in life.

Braydon's grin widened as he swung into the saddle and his horse fell into step next to Brody's. "I got your back, brother."

Yuma was nearly an hour's ride northeast of Bullet. On the far side of town lay Hawkes's spread, the largest parcel of land in the county owned by one man alone. Most of the folks hereabouts knew Hawkes had expanded his holdings through ill-gotten means, but few were willing or able to stand up against a man who controlled almost the entire county, including the sheriff's department.

Brody felt his gut tighten as they drew close. The ranch house was barely visible in the distance, sprawling as it did in the dustbowl desert landscape. Everything on the spread was kept orderly by a group of Mexican workers that Hawkes drove like slaves.

Like everything in Hawkes's life, the workers were disposable. Brody doubted Hawkes even had loyalty to his own son. Rumor had it Hawkes killed his wife in a fit of jealous rage when she tried to leave him.

"Look away, brother," Braydon said at his side. "His time will come. We'll see to that."

Brody just grunted and picked up the pace. He tended to get antsy anytime he was away from the ranch for long. He knew more about the ranch and its secrets than the rest of them could even dream of.

Reaching Yuma, they stopped in front of the gambling hall just off Main Street where Brody knew there was almost always a high-stakes poker game in a back room. Admittance was closely controlled. Sure enough, one of the thugs on the door nodded at Brody but shook his head at Braydon.

"Just you, man. He stays out here."

Braydon looked unperturbed. "I'll be in the saloon next door."

Brody nodded over his shoulder as the door closed behind him. He didn't anticipate any trouble.

IN AN EFFORT TO stop thinking about Brody, Laura decided it was time she got her affairs in order. She planned to be in Bullet for a while, so she needed to open a bank account which meant a trip to Yuma and the nearest branch of the Savings and Loan. She had brought cash with her, but no one needed to know she was more than wealthy in her own right. Let them think she was dependent on her meagre earnings as a school teacher, carefully banking her pay and living frugally.

As her borrowed carriage and horse rolled along, her gaze flitted toward the river, close to the place where Brody used to take her. She returned her gaze to the road ahead. Was she even now traveling the same road where Pa and her brother Royston beat Brody to a pulp that fateful night before her father packed up the family and headed north?

Laura had known leaving was for the best. Despite her denouncing Brody in front of the entire congregation of Yuma, she wasn't convinced he'd stay away. Next time her Pa caught Brody near her he'd more than likely kill him.

She loved Brody too much to let that happen.

In no time she was seated across the desk from the somber-looking manager at Yuma Savings and Loan. "I'm just new to the area myself," Laura said chattily. "How about you—" she took a closer look at his name tag, "—Mr. Lawry?"

The poor gentleman blushed to the roots of his visibly thinning hair but managed to stammer out, "This is my first year."

Laura relaxed. What she did *not* want was to run into someone who recalled the Kismet family from hereabouts ten years earlier.

Mr. Lawry cleared his throat. "Will your husband be coming in as well?"

"I don't believe that is necessary any longer, by law." This type of treatment never happened to her in California, but she guessed a woman alone opening an account didn't happen often in Arizona, even though it was now legal in most states. Recently, a woman in New York City had opened a stock exchange solely for women speculating on railroad stocks.

"Of course not," he stammered. "I was just asking."

Laura smiled sweetly. "It will be just myself banking here."

"Yes, ma'am." Once the paperwork had been drawn up and signed, Laura was torn between a desire to see what other changes had been wrought in her girlhood town, and putting distance between her past and her present. But first she planned to check on her old friend, Miss Hinkle, and see if the old dear was still alive. Sadly, she learned the woman had passed on five years earlier.

She avoided the side of town where her family home still stood. Even then, everywhere she looked brought back memories of Brody. She crossed the town square where she used to wait for him faithfully. She could still recall the way he rode down Main Street on that big old horse of his, grinning ear-to-ear as soon as he caught sight of her.

Speaking of Brody—.

Was that him stepping out of the gaming hall across the street? In the company of another man? She blew out a breath. Of course he was still gambling. Some things never change.

Why should she feel relieved he wasn't in the company of a woman? She must have stared a few moments too long, for the second man caught her gaze on them and a flicker of interest crossed his features. He said something to Brody who turned his head her way.

She felt as if she'd been shot through with lightning. Her and Brody in Yuma. It could have been yesterday. Except it wasn't.

To her dismay, the man with Brody started to cross the street, leaving Brody no choice but to follow.

The man reached her side in long, purposeful strides and whisked his hat from his head. "I do declare, if my eyes are not deceiving me, it is Bullet's very own new school teacher here on her own in Yuma. I'm Braydon Mason, and this is my brother, Brody."

"Your brother and I are already acquainted," Laura said stiffly.

Braydon cocked a look Brody's way. "Well, well. You never said a word, Brody. Please introduce me to the comely new schoolmarm."

"Braydon, meet Miss Kismet."

Laura couldn't stop the small, shivery thrill that rushed through her as Brody spoke.

"As you may have judged, Braydon is the shy one of my brothers."

Braydon guffawed and punched him in the arm. "Always a kidder, Brody. And always did play them close to your chest." He turned his attentions back to Laura. "I wasn't aware Brody had been lucky enough to be the first Mason to welcome you to Bullet."

"Actually," Laura started to say, then bit off her words. She had asked Brody not to share their previous acquaintance. "Actually, it's a pleasure to meet you, Braydon. I don't know that I'd describe my recent meeting with Brody as exactly welcoming."

"He can be that way," Braydon said, with a conspiratorial grin. "Don't take it personally. We'll have to invite you out to the ranch one night for supper, won't we now, Brody? Show Miss Kismet a right friendly Bullet-style welcome. In the meantime, perhaps we can accompany you to the tearoom in the next block?"

She didn't miss the way Brody's eyes shot daggers at his brother. Clearly, he had no more wish to be in her company than she in his.

"Such a kind offer. Sadly, I must decline. I need to head back and pack up my things. I'm moving tomorrow." *That* got Brody rattled.

"Leaving Bullet so soon?" he asked.

Was he hopeful or disappointed? She couldn't tell. "Nothing of the sort. I've imposed long enough on the hospitality of my employer."

Braydon nodded. "Did set a few tongues wagging. You living at Hawkes's place when you first came to town."

"Someone should open a decent hotel," Laura said, primly.

Brody spoke up. "Doesn't really seem a need, what with the rail line stopping here in Yuma."

"Anything could happen. Gold or oil could be discovered and Bullet turn into a boom town."

Brody glowered. "Don't see that coming on."

Laura gave him a closer look. She knew him well, or had

once. Seemed a pretty strong reaction to what she only meant as a passing remark.

"I'll bid you good day, gentleman. Don't let me keep you from the calling of the cards."

She was out of earshot before Braydon spoke. "What did she mean by that? It's like she knows you take part in a game from time to time."

Brody shrugged. "Lucky guess. You were doing such a good job of being the charmer. How about you take over the wager to woo her away from Hawkes?"

"Not a chance. I'd say you met your match with that one. I can't wait for the next installment."

CHAPTER 3

Laura made good time on the drive back to the Hawkes ranch. Bypassing the ranch house, she steered the borrowed rig directly into the massive wood-timbered stable.

As she was climbing down from her seat, she heard the rumbling rise and fall of masculine voices coming from the tack room. Curiously she edged closer, careful to stay in the shadows.

"I don't think we need to worry about Mason anymore, Boss."

"What do you mean? He's still strutting around. All of them are. I told you to poison that branch of the river, not just redirect it. I want results, damn it." Hawkes's voice dropped lower and took on a menacing tone.

"What you don't want is anything that brings the law breathing down your neck," came the placating response.

"I can take care of the law!" Hawkes's voice rose to a bellow.

"And I can take care of the Masons. Come tax time,

Mason won't have enough scratch for his own taxes, never mind be funding his neighbors."

"I need to own that land!" Hawkes roared.

"So you keep saying. Makes a fellow wonder what's so darn special about that particular tract." The stranger's voice had taken on a speculative tone.

"It's not just Mason's." Hawkes sounded calmer, as if realizing he'd reacted too strongly. "Got myself some serious plans for that entire area. And that's all you need to know. Now do what I pay you for and don't come back till it's done."

Laura pressed herself into the shadows as a strange man strode past, his hat pulled low over his face, obscuring his features. As he left, she rushed back to the buggy and made like she was just climbing down as Hawkes came out of the tack room.

From the corner of her eye she saw his big meaty hand reach out as if to steady her, and side-stepped from his touch.

"Thank you, but I'm just fine, Mr. Hawkes."

"Now, now Laura. Haven't I told you time and again to call me Guy? Mr. Hawkes was my pa."

"I just don't feel right about being on a first name basis with my employer is all." She cast her eyes down to the hay-strewn floor. She couldn't bear to look at him. What was he up to regarding Brody's ranch?

"I'd like you to think of me as a friend, as well as an employer. You being new in town and all." She felt the sting of his lascivious look, which left her in need of a basin of water and a strong scrubbing brush.

"I'm quite looking forward to next week and getting the chance to meet the children and their families. I wish I knew how many to expect and their ages. It would make my lesson planning easier."

"You leave that to old Guy. I have friends in high places. Shouldn't take much to get that information."

"Thank you." She turned to make her way out of the barn, toward the sprawling ranch house.

His words followed her and she felt her back stiffen. "See you at supper. You wear something pretty now, you hear?"

Once inside Laura went in search of the housekeeper, a sad-faced Mexican woman named Isabela. Laura had thought, if she was staying longer, she might convince Isabela to confide why she always looked so sad. Even now, dust rag in hand in the great hall, the other woman's eyes were haunted.

"Isabela, I'm in need of my valise. Do you know where it is?"

"Si, Señorita. Mr. Guy, he take it."

"Take it where?"

Isabela shrugged one plump shoulder.

"But I need it," Laura said, frustrated. "You must have some idea where it is."

"Where what is, lovely Laura?"

She turned to face Hawkes but not before she saw a shadow of fear and despair cross Isabela's face.

"Leave us," Hawkes snapped at Isabela. The house-keeper skittled off like a frightened hare.

Laura straightened her shoulders and faced her host. "My valise. It's not in my room where I left it."

She stood her ground as Hawkes brushed a strand of hair back off her shoulder. His fingers reminded her of sausages hanging in a butcher's window. "Petite little thing like you. I didn't want you tripping over it and maybe getting hurt."

Right, Laura thought. She always tripped on things stowed beneath her bed.

She lifted her chin and met his smarmy gaze. "I was going to tell you at supper, but I see no point in waiting until then. I require my valise as I will be packing my things in it tonight. Tomorrow I plan to move to town where I'm closer to the school."

His eyes narrowed in his fleshy face, bushy gray brows drawn together in a straight line. "Something lacking with our hospitality? It's been a long time since Jeffrey and I have enjoyed the sight of a pretty face across the table. Isn't that right, son?" His voice rose at the last, as if Jeffrey might be hard of hearing.

She hadn't seen Jeffrey slink in, but that didn't surprise her. He tended to creep about as if he hoped no one, particularly his father, noticed he was there.

Jeffrey cleared his throat, something Laura noticed he did a lot when in the presence of his father. "What's that, Father?"

"Laura here tells me she plans to move out tomorrow. I say that's a right shame, don't you?"

"Indeed." Jeffrey caught her hand. "I beg you to reconsider." There was an element of panic in his voice that led her to conclude Jeffrey had no wish to be alone with his father in a house that was far too big for the two of them.

Laura gently disengaged his hold. "You two both surely know how to turn a girl's head. You have made me feel so welcome here in Bullet and in your home. But truly, it is better I reside closer to town. I have imposed long enough."

"I hope you're not letting the gossipy old biddies in town get to you," Hawkes said.

"Not at all. I'm afraid I'm somewhat of a modern woman who values her independence. I got quite used to living on my own in Los Angeles."

Hawkes narrowed his eyes to mean little slits. His voice changed from smooth-talker to that of a bully. "You're not in California, little lady. And I'll remind you of the contract you signed the day you showed up here. A school teacher's morals need to be above reproach. Need to withstand the scrutiny of the good folks of Bullet who are trusting their children to your influence."

"I *am* thinking about my reputation," Laura said. "What I hear is the good people of Bullet are looking askance at my living here with two unmarried men."

"No one would dare—" Hawkes spat out.

"You might control this town. You don't control how people think," Laura said.

She watched as Hawkes's face turned several mottled shades of red before he hissed out a breath. Appearing noticeably calmer, he changed his approach. "Well now, I never looked at it from that point of view. You might be right. We need to find you a suitable place."

"I've already found a situation, thank you."

"Suitable to the education board, I mean."

"I understood *you* to be the education board."

"Well now, that's true enough. Means I have to approve your place of residence. And, of course, see that you adhere to your curfew."

"Curfew?"

"School teacher can't be out sashaying around town. Need to set an example." His self-satisfied smile returned. "Need a man's protection as well. Woman on her own, never know what folks take to saying or thinking. You leave it to me, little Laura. I'll find you a suitable place."

Deflated, Laura made her way upstairs to the guest wing.

The second Laura was out of earshot, Hawkes turned on his useless son. "I hope you learned a lesson from this; bringing an ungrateful, unpredictable stranger into our town and into our home. Just 'cause you're sweet on her."

Jeffrey sounded resigned. "I thought you would be pleased, Father. But clearly there is no way of my ever doing anything that meets your exacting standards."

"Growing some balls would be a good start." Hawkes cackled at his own wit. "You just wait till I get the report on Miss High-and-Mighty from that detective. We'll see who has the exacting standards."

"I told you hiring a detective wasn't necessary," Jeffrey said stiffly, before he turned on his heel.

Hawkes watched him go. Jeffrey knew squat. Hawkes planned to keep it that way.

"DAYS ARE GETTING SHORTER," Braydon observed to Brody as they traveled back to the ranch from Yuma.

Brody made some murmured response, but he was only listening with half an ear. Each time he saw Laura, it was more and more difficult to erase her from his thoughts.

Instead, he tried to focus on what Braydon was saying about the weather. Not that there was much of a seasonal change in Arizona. It tended to shift from hot and dry to really hot and dry, interspersed with the occasional monsoon that emptied the heavens and caused flood water to run in rivulets over the parched desert-like land. They were lucky to be on the river with the ability to irrigate a small tract of land where they grew most of their food, as well as a plentiful supply of water for the cattle and other livestock.

Reaching Copper Moon, the two men headed for the barn and saw to their horses before making their way to the house. "How long you figure till the next herd is ready for delivery to the west?" Brody asked.

"I reckon a month or more," Braydon said. "Why?"

"An idea I've been working on, now that the railroad crosses the river."

Braydon cocked his head. "You thinking of moving the cattle by rail?"

"Times are changing," Brody said. "Best we change with them. We can manage with only a couple of us to move the cattle west by railcar while the others head down to Mexico and bring back the next herd."

Braydon nodded. "You figure we can double our output of mature head out west."

"They're hungry for our beef. Might as well keep 'em satisfied."

"You're not worried it might leave the ranch more vulnerable?"

Brody didn't want to go there. "No more vulnerable than in the past."

"You seem pretty het up with the railroad," Braydon said. "You sink some capital into it?"

Brody hesitated, then nodded. "We can't rely solely on cattle. It seemed like a good place to diversify."

"You've got the head for business," Braydon said.

"And you've got the head for the ladies."

Bishop caught Brody's last remark as they entered the ranch house. "Braydon charming the ladies again? I thought he was along to watch your back, Brody."

"One lady in particular," Braydon said, ignoring Brody's 'shut up' look. "Who'd we run into in Yuma but Bullet's own little schoolmarm, name of Miss Laura Kismet. Seems Brody has already launched his plans for charming the lady away from Hawkes."

Blake's gaze flew to Brody. "Miss Laura Kismet? *The* Laura Kismet?"

Brody sat down with a heavy sigh. Trust Blake. He might not be able to read but he had a memory like a steel trap. "The same."

Benjamin spoke up. "I don't get it."

"Me either," Braydon chimed in.

Which meant the rest of them didn't remember that day Laura had shown up at the ranch looking for him.

"You going to tell us what this is all about?" Bradley said.

"It's Brody's story to tell," Blake said.

"It's not a big deal," Brody said. "Turns out the school teacher and I met years back. Matter of fact, that's where the barn cat, Smoky, came from."

"Sweet on her, were you?" chimed in Barron, with a teasing smile.

"All's I know is her pa didn't cotton to me much."

"What? Not good enough for his little girl?" Braydon said.

Brody took his time answering. No one knew it was the Kismet men who had beat him within an inch of his life. Or the fact that Laura had denounced him in front of what felt like the entire town of Yuma. Some things a man was better keeping to himself.

"Heard tell the family got gold fever and moved to Black Hills. Never gave her another thought until I recognized her the other day at the schoolhouse."

The brothers fell silent. Blake knew more of the story than the rest. Brody preferred it stay that way.

"Think she came back to town hoping to pick up where you two left off?" Barron would think that.

Brody snorted. "She wasn't the least bit happy to see me the other day. Braydon will back that up with our run-in today. I think someone else needs to take over the wooing of the fair schoolmarm."

"She didn't seem over-pleased when we saw her in Yuma," Braydon agreed. "Said their initial meeting hadn't been very welcoming."

"What did she expect?" Brody barked. "I had no idea it was her. Caught me off guard, is what."

"I think Braydon is right." Bradley gave him a cocky look. "I say Miss Laura Kismet is open game. Pull out all your stops and may the best man win."

Brody blanched. "Wait a minute, now. See here—"

"Aren't afraid of a little friendly competition are you Brody? Feel like you got prior claim on the lady, do you?" Braydon teased.

"No such thing," Brody blustered.

"Seems to me, if we're going to turn her interest from Hawkes, we need to show her a little Mason hospitality." This from Benjamin.

"I did invite her out to the ranch for supper," Braydon said.

"Slow down there," said Bradley. "Give the rest of us a chance to catch up."

The words swirled around Brody as the brothers schemed and boasted and egged each other on as to how and when to best win the school teacher's favor.

"Aren't you forgetting one thing?" Brody said. "Two

things actually. One, the lady is living under Hawkes's roof. Two, none of you knows squat about wooing a woman."

"She did say she's moving closer to town," Braydon said helpfully.

"I'll wager we know as much about wooing a lady as you do. Maybe even more," said one of the twins.

Across the room he saw Blake's sympathetic gaze on him. He immediately rose and shook it off. He wasn't in the mood for sympathy. Blake knew what Laura had once meant to him. What Blake didn't know is that time had not lessened those feelings one bit. Despite the quickening of his heart when she was around, he knew Laura was not what she seemed. And not a woman to be trusted.

He dragged his weary body off to bed, leaving the others to their wagers and schemes about wooing the fair lady's hand. Anything that got her away from under Hawkes's evil thumb was a good thing. Or so he tried to convince himself.

TRUE TO FORM, Hawkes did not relinquish Laura's valise. Dinner had been a strained affair. After retiring, she tossed and turned most of the night, berating herself for being in such a hurry to help Brody that she had not read the contract thoroughly. And of course, Hawkes had the only copy.

No doubt he would alter it to suit his needs. Including where she lived and what sort of curfew she was subject to. Should she blatantly disregard the contract, she would be dismissed before she even started work.

Would that be such a bad thing? Being under the evil eye of Hawkes sounded imminently worse. Although without access to his plan of attack against Brody's ranch, she was as good as useless here.

Since Hawkes hadn't yet revoked any privileges, she helped herself to the rig she'd been driving and headed to see Amanda and give her the bad news.

Amanda had obviously been waiting for her and raced down the front steps before Laura had alighted.

Amanda pulled up short at the sight of the empty buggy. Her face fell. "Change your mind so soon?"

Laura clambered down. "Hawkes maintains the education board has to approve my living arrangements."

Amanda rocked back on her heels. "You can't have that. He'll either keep you prisoner at his place or farm you out with the local pastor and his wife. Both bad ideas."

"I don't want there to be repercussions to you and your mother if you help me cross him."

"Won't make no difference. Ma's been crossing him all her life. You have him over a barrel, you know."

"I don't follow."

"School's set to open in a few days," Amanda said. "Hawkes been full of himself, prattling on about the great thing he's done for Bullet. If he fires you, he's stuck for a teacher and he looks bad to the townsfolk. Nothing that man hates more than losing face."

"Unless it's being opposed. I hate to think what he might do in retaliation," Laura said.

"Trust me," Amanda said. "He needs you more than you need him."

Laura pondered her options. It was untenable to stay under Hawkes's roof. If she left, she at least stood a chance to pump Jeffrey for information without his father eyeing her every move.

"You're right," she said at last. "Let him dismiss me if he

chooses. It won't curry favor with the parents looking forward to their children's chance for an education."

IT DIDN'T TAKE LONG for word to spread around Bullet and out to Copper Moon Ranch that the new school teacher had thumbed her nose at Hawkes and his 'rules'. Not only had she chosen her own place to live, she fully intended to pay little mind to the curfew Hawkes tried to impose on her. Folks murmured among themselves, wondering just how long she might last.

Brody wondered that as well. Laura had no idea what she was getting into opposing Hawkes so publicly. He needed to warn her.

Thanks to his brothers taking up the slack in project 'wooing Laura', it would be damn near impossible to get her alone. Personally, Brody thought the entire ruse was unnecessary. It would appear Laura had snubbed Hawkes to the point where he no longer had a yen for her. Or would the old man's ire make him all the more eager to control Laura?

He hated that he was reduced to spying on her. Made him no better than the Hawkes men. But when he saw her leave the café and make her way toward the livery, he fell into step a ways behind. He ducked inside the livery after her, giving his eyes a chance to adjust from the full-on sunlight outside, to the dim interior. Like every barn he'd ever been in, it had that familiar odor of hay and horseflesh underscored by leather and manure.

Somewhere ahead he heard the rise and fall of her familiar, sweet voice as she spoke to someone, but he couldn't make out what was being said. He hovered near the entrance.

Before long, the owner came out leading a pretty dappled gray, followed by Laura. The two were chatting and laughing, too busy to notice Brody in the shadows behind a post. He felt a stab of resentment at the way the other fellow held the horse and spoke in far too familiar a fashion to Laura as she mounted and took the reins from him.

As soon as she started off, he sprinted over to where he'd left Phoenix. From what he could tell, it appeared she was headed toward the park near the river.

HAWKES EYEBALLED the man seated across his desk from him. Sir Percival Bloom was somewhat of a dandy, but then maybe all Englishmen acted the same. Last thing he needed was this jackass snooping around, possibly digging up things that were best left buried. Hawkes had too much riding on his latest project to risk having it derailed by some so-called treasure hunter.

"I make it a point," Bloom was saying. "Anytime I enter a new community, I make my intention known to the folks who matter. Around these parts, that would be you, Mr. Hawkes."

Hawkes ignored the man's blatant attempt at flattery. "It's true I have friends in the right places. And a certain vested interest in several aspects of prosperity for our fair town. I'll tell you straight, Bloom, I think you're wasting everyone's time here. There's no more a ship full of pearls buried in the sand than there's a man in the moon."

"All I want is your blessing as I conduct more research," Percy said.

"As I understand, you'll be starting the far side of town. Near the border," Hawkes said.

"That's the initial place I want to get started," Percy said. "And naturally for any assistance I receive from you, there would be a substantial 'finder's fee' at the project's end."

Hawkes didn't bite. No find meant no fee. And he had no intention of seeing the man's project succeed. But Bloom was no dummy. If Hawkes spoke out too adamantly against the whole idea, he'd pique Sir Percy's curiosity as to what Hawkes might prefer stay undiscovered in the area in question.

"Might find yourself in a bit of opposition from the Masons," Hawkes said. "Those boys are difficult at the best of times." He leaned forward across the desk in a gesture of fake friendship. "Tell you what? How's about I have a little chat with them. On your behalf."

"That would be most appreciated," Sir Percy said.

"Good." Hawkes stood. "Consider it done."

Percy stood as well. "Very good, Sir."

"Oh, and Bloom. One more thing—"

BRODY FOLLOWED Laura from a discreet distance. As he thought, the town park proved to be her destination. The area was deserted at this hour, as most folks were home preparing their evening meal.

A slight breeze from the river cooled the air just enough to make it feel almost pleasant. Irrigation provided a near-lush look to the green space, which surrounded the jewel in the crown, a sparkly white gazebo built last year by local volunteers.

Brody kept Laura in his sights as she reined to a stop near the gazebo. She appeared to be looking around. Was she meeting someone? His jaw clenched at the thought of Laura with another man.

Gracefully she dismounted and turned toward where he stood, partially obscured behind some spindly bushes close to the road. "Why are you following me, Brody?"

CHAPTER 4

Laura shifted her weight from one foot to the other. Who did Brody think he was fooling? He was never far from her thoughts, and whenever he was close something triggered her awareness. She had been aware of him the second he set foot in the livery. And every minute he followed her here.

As he stepped toward her from the camouflaging brush, she willed her rapidly beating heart to slow.

"I was worried about you," he said.

"Do you mind telling me why?"

"Word around town is how you thumbed your nose at Hawkes. He's not a man who takes kindly to being crossed."

"From what I've seen, he's not a man who takes kindly to much."

Brody seemed to straighten and grow taller right before her eyes. "I'd never forgive myself if something happened to you."

Laura felt the fight go out of her. Why would she even want to fight him? She had loved him since their first run-in, when he had literally knocked her off her feet.

"I feel the same. I know it's not much comfort, but that's why I denounced you all those years ago. If you tangled with Pa and Royston a second time, I'd be here leaving flowers on your grave." She gave her head a sorrowful shake. "Seemed at the time like the only choice I had."

She saw the conflicted feelings shadowing his gaze. Did he still care? Would he ever forgive her?

"We always have choices, Laura."

"Do we?" She notched up her chin in a challenging stance.

"Don't always make the right one," Brody said. "Even if it seems like it at the time."

She could tell from the way he stared off into the distance that he was thinking about times past.

"And no way to undo what's already done," she said. She felt the pitch of tension stir the air between them.

"How about starting over?" he said, finally. "Pretend we never met before. You're new in town. I'm offering to show you the sights."

Her heart quickened in hope, then crumpled in despair. How could they possibly forget the past? Forget what they had once meant to each other.

"I loved you once. It tore me apart to lose you. I don't know that I would recover from that pain a second time."

She could tell he didn't like her answer. His stance stiffened. He stared out over her head, a muscle working in his jaw. His Adam's apple bobbed as if he was having trouble swallowing.

"Seems as if your mind is already made up," he said tightly. "So why did you come back here? And not some pat answer, Laura. The truth. It's me, remember."

As if she could forget. Not his touch, his taste, his smell. Anything. She weighed her options. Tell him the truth and have him order her away. Maybe even expose her true motive to Hawkes, rendering her presence here useless.

Childishly, she crossed her fingers behind her back. "I met Jeffrey when he was in California. I fancied him. He made me homesick for the area. When he told me about the teaching job, it gave me not just a chance to move back, but a chance for a better life."

Brody's eyes narrowed. "Money is what brought you here?"

Laura bit her bottom lip. Lying to Brody was more difficult than she had expected. "I'm used to nice things, Brody. Nicer than anything you could provide. If that sounds mercenary, then so be it. I'm past the age of being labeled a spinster. Which changes if I make a good match."

"Jeffrey is nothing but a puppet for his old man."

"You don't know him the way I do. We spent quite a bit of time together in Los Angeles. I enjoyed living in the big house when I got here. Then I realized that moving out the way I did should force Jeffrey to do the right thing. To move me back in as the new Mrs. Hawkes."

Disgust washed over Brody's face. Laura let out a pent-up breath. He believed her.

"Don't think that by marrying Jeffrey, you'll be guaranteed the old man's protection. Marriage didn't do a thing to help Jeffrey's mother."

LAURA ACCOMPANIED Amanda to church on Sunday where her new friend's piano music was joined by the voices of the choir and parishioners. Several of the congregation stopped on their way out to welcome Laura to Bullet. She sensed reticence and caution behind the words of welcome.

Only old Mrs. Delaney, the town postmistress, spoke her mind. "Folks is happy you're here, Miss Kismet. But they won't be taking sides against himself." Her sharp gaze slid from Laura to Amanda and back to Laura. "Might not have been seemly to be living out there with two gentlemen, but two ladies living alone with no man to protect them has folks taking exception just the same."

Amanda spoke up. "Ma and I been on our own since I was a baby. Ain't no reason for the townsfolk to have their knickers in a twist."

"Everyone hereabouts needs to see to their own needs. You know that," Mrs. Delaney said as she took her leave.

Amanda exchanged glances with Laura. "She means they're afraid of Hawkes, even if on the surface they appear to support whatever he's about."

"How does he drive such fear into the townsfolk?" Laura wondered aloud.

Amanda shrugged. "From time to time some brave soul opposes Hawkes and his power-hungry ways, only to have bad things happen. Or never be seen again."

Laura wondered if that's what happened to Jeffrey's mother. Did the woman oppose her husband and pay for it with her life?

Laura turned to Amanda. "Why isn't your mother afraid of him like everyone else?"

"Don't rightly know. Figure she must have something powerful over him. Whatever it is, he stays clear."

As they rounded the corner and approached the Cooke house, Laura stopped short. The front steps sheltered a small bounty of gifts. Fresh eggs alongside a loaf of fresh-baked bread and a covered casserole. Amanda flung her arm round Laura's shoulder. "Looks to me like the new school teacher is a hit."

"Are you serious? I haven't even done anything yet. This can't all be for me."

"Folks showing their approval is all," Amanda said.

Neither of them paid any attention to the sounds of a horse and rider approaching until man and beast pulled up and slowed alongside them. The man reached down and handed Laura a bouquet of wildflowers, doffing his Stetson as he did so. "Welcome to Bullet, Miss Kismet." Then he straightened, replaced his hat on his head and resumed his travels.

Laura stood staring after him with her mouth hanging open, then turned to Amanda. "Who was that?"

"One of the Mason brothers. I dare say you have yourself an admirer. Come on. Help me with this other stuff."

Neither of them noticed Jeffrey Hawkes watching them from across the street.

So, one of the Masons was taken with the fair school teacher was he? Jeffrey would be putting a stop to that. His father had told him to keep an eye on Laura, a task Jeffrey was more than happy to undertake. While Hawkes Sr. waited on the report he'd commissioned from the private detective, he wanted to know Laura's every move.

No need for his father to know about Mason's visit. As for the rest of the gifts, he'd placed those on the steps while the ladies were at church, in an attempt to lull lovely Laura into a false sense of acceptance by the town.

If their fair school teacher had an ulterior motive for her time here in Bullet, his father would find out what it was. Except that Jeffrey planned to beat him to it. It was far past time someone beat the old man at his own game.

~

Brody was still smarting over Laura's claim that she was here because of financial security. Had thrown her lot in with Jeffrey Hawkes for the same reason.

Not that any of her chatter had a thing to do with his visit today to the gambling halls in Yuma. From an early age, he had learned that money could buy a lot of things, including power. He'd just never considered it a means to owning the lifetime affections of a lady.

Not that he was trying to amass financial success as a lure to get Laura back. Nothing of the sort. But affluence meant more than survival around here. It was a necessary part of his intent to destroy Hawkes.

Several hours later he sat with a healthy stack of winnings in front of him as the dealer shuffled the cards, when the game was interrupted by the door opening to admit a newcomer.

"New player, gentlemen," said the armed guard, who decided who was granted admittance to the back room where the serious money was being wagered.

The dealer set down the cards. Brody glanced over his shoulder and did a double-take at the sight of his sworn enemy, strolling into the room as if he owned the place. He stared straight ahead, aware Hawkes hadn't yet looked his way. Brody knew that, despite appearances to the contrary, Hawkes couldn't afford the kind of stakes they were playing for. Which meant his day just got a whole lot more interesting.

"Good day, gents." Hawkes pulled out an empty chair. "Hear there's some high stakes being wagered. Appreciate you all letting me join in." Slowly, his gaze circled the table as he spoke. Brody kept his face impassable, waiting.

It didn't take but a moment. Hawkes's gaze skipped over him, then backed up for a second look. Immediately, the man's entire demeanor changed. His eyes narrowed to slits, as if he couldn't believe what he was seeing. His whole body grew stiff as he pushed himself back to his feet.

"'Fraid I changed my mind. I don't sit with no cheaters."

The man on Brody's left reached for his gun. "Who you be calling a cheater?"

Brody placed a hand on the other fellow's arm. "If you happen to be looking my way, Hawkes, not a man in the room will back you up. They know I play fair."

Hawkes huffed out a breath. "Guess none of them know what I know. How the apple didn't fall far from the tree. How you're a bigger liar and cheat than your old man. And that's saying a mouthful."

Hawkes glanced around the table, as if seeking support. "Don't be fooled by Mason's holier-than-thou talk. His old man was the biggest cheat on the circuit back in the day. Right up till I put an end to it."

Brody felt his fists clench. Some of the men here were new to him. A few, for certain, resented his recent winning streak. Would they believe Hawkes?

With a casualness he was far from feeling, he said, "You and I have never sat down together to a game." Not that he had any intention of ever sitting across a deck of cards from Hawkes. But he couldn't appear bothered by the other man's bluster.

"That's 'cause I know better. I expected a quality game today. Appears folks around here need to be more selective who they let join in." Hawkes made a big deal of slamming the door behind him on his way out.

Brody looked around, aware all eyes rested on him.

"Any truth to what he said?" asked one grizzled old player.

"Heck, no. He took one look at the competition and

knew he was way over his head," Brody said. "Are we here to play cards or what?"

The dealer pushed a fresh deck his way. "Your turn to cut."

The sun was starting to set by the time Brody hit the saddle and headed for home. He'd been extra careful with his moves today, after Hawkes's little tirade, so it took that much longer before he had enough winnings to cash out.

"Can't believe they put up with you so long."

Brody felt the hair rise on the back of his neck as Hawkes voice cut toward him from the shadows across the street. The words were slurred, which meant Hawkes had spent most of the day in the saloon. Probably playing for chump change and stewing that he wasn't in with the serious players.

He spun Phoenix in a circle, just as Hawkes appeared. Past times it had been Hawkes mounted, looking down on Brody. Tonight, he took satisfaction from the reversal of roles. Him looking down on Hawkes for a change. Him with the serious players while Hawkes pecked at leftover crumbs.

"Lose your horse?" he inquired mildly. He wished it was true. He'd go buy the beast immediately, at any price, just to lord it over the man.

Which is when he got a grip. He couldn't go losing his focus. This game he was embroiled in was a long game. Nothing to be gained from meaningless triumphs along the way which, while they might assuage his ego, distracted from the end prize.

"I ought to shoot you down in cold blood, same as I did your useless pa," Hawkes said.

Brody saw the way the other man couldn't even stand straight, and doubted he could hit the broad side of anything at the moment.

"'Cept I won't," Hawkes said. "I got something better planned for you. You and those miserable saps leaching off your uncle's ranch, with no idea the true riches they're sitting atop." He laughed uproariously. "Can just see it now. Everyone wondering what happened to poor old Mason and his misfits."

Hawkes drew closer as he spoke. Something about the measured lurch of each step signaled a warning. Hawkes wasn't drunk. He just wanted Brody to think he was. Brody dug his heels into Phoenix's flanks. The horse leapt forward and Brody missed the lasso that whistled through the air toward him.

He heard Hawkes behind him, swearing at his goons. Beneath him, Phoenix picked up on the urgency of them beating a hasty retreat back to the ranch.

Laura found the first day of school draining, as they always were. Not only were the students full of nervous energy, the older ones were constantly testing her as to the firmness of her rule.

Between a nervous first-timer wetting his pants, two older boys having a spit ball fight, a timid first grader bursting into tears from time to time, and one student's lunch going missing, it had been a full day. By the time Laura had cleaned up spit balls, swept the floor and emptied the trash all she wanted to do was go home to the Cooke house and soak in a nice hot bath.

She packed up the books she needed to take home to prepare the next day's lessons and stepped outside into the blistering afternoon heat. Her wide-brimmed bonnet offered scant protection from the intense sunlight as she shifted her books more comfortably into the crook of her other elbow.

"Howdy, Miss Kismet." A lanky cowboy stepped into view. "Let me help you with those books."

She was too shocked to stop him from scooping them from her grip as he extended his free hand her way. "Blake Mason, Miss. Don't like to see a pretty lady walking home alone."

She gave him a curious look, aware he was not the same Mason brother who had shown up yesterday with the flowers. Was Blake the one Brody said was unable to learn to read?

"My landlady has already warned me about you Mason men," she said primly, as he fell into step alongside her and shortened his long stride to match hers. "I would think you would have your work cut out for you on the ranch, without chasing into town to keep a watch over me. Unless you have a yen to rile up Guy Hawkes more than he's already riled."

"Just doing our civic duty," Mason said. "My brother, Benjamin, stopped by yesterday to say 'how do'. Happened to see Jeffrey Hawkes skulking across the way. He's probably watching you right this second, on orders from the old man. Junior doesn't seem to do much thinking for himself."

"Is it wise to ruffle Hawkes's feathers?" She cringed, hearing her own words. "I wasn't meaning that to be funny."

He gave her a long, admiring look. "You tell me. Is it wise?"

"I would wager you have a lot more at stake than I do. I can always get another teaching job."

"We Masons don't cotton much to bullies."

"So I've heard," Laura said primly.

"Oh, I believe you know, Miss Kismet. First hand, from back in the day when you first knew Brody."

"Is that what this is about?" she asked, stung. "Brody sent you to keep an eye on me?"

"No, Miss. Matter of fact, he's dead set against it."

Laura felt herself start to deflate, and buoyed herself up with difficulty. Silly, to have harbored hope that Brody might still have feelings for her. "So now you're riling up Brody as well."

They both slowed their steps as they reached the Cooke house.

Blake passed her back her books. "Oh, I think Brody was riled up plenty, Miss. Soon as he saw you'd shown up in town."

CHAPTER 5

Thus began a routine Laura didn't look forward to but was powerless to stop. Each day after school, one or another of the Mason brothers appeared to walk her home, often bringing her a small gift: a sweet or cold drink or nosegay of flowers. Amanda found it amusing until the time Bradley Mason was her companion.

"Don't see why you need every last one of the Masons swooning at your feet," Amanda groused, polishing the piano so vigorously Laura wouldn't have been surprised to see the finish wiped clear off the wood.

"It's not like that," Laura said.

"You say." Amanda continued to torture the top of the piano, until Laura grabbed her arm.

"Listen to me," Laura said. "Blake let it slip that the brothers all drew straws to try and woo me, in case Hawkes had me in his sights. Brody got the short straw, but he didn't know it was me till he showed up at the schoolhouse. Right after that, he washed his hands and left it to the others. Seems they're all having a go."

Amanda furrowed her brow. "Why would Brody do that?"

Laura bit her lip. It seemed the Masons all knew about her history with Brody. Which didn't mean Amanda needed to know as well. Bullet was far too gossipy.

"Didn't think much of me, I suppose. Haven't seen him at all. It's been the others coming around. On top of which, Jeffrey has been hanging about, not making his presence known, just lurking in the shadows."

Amanda looked out the window. "Something which appears about to change."

Laura peered over her friend's shoulder to see Jeffrey Hawkes was indeed standing on the porch with his hand raised. Even his knock was timid. Amanda gave Laura a push toward the door. As she opened it, Jeffrey removed his hat and made a sweeping bow.

"Good day," he said, perspiration beading his upper lip. He really was very plain-looking compared to the tall, dark-haired Mason brothers. Poor Jeffrey's light brown hair was thinning on top. His chin was weak and decidedly fleshy. He had his father's sausage-shaped fingers, although none of the meanness Laura had seen in Hawkes Senior's eyes. Jeffrey was just a poor, harmless man with a bully of a father.

"Hello, Jeffrey," Laura said, a question in her voice.

"Lovely Laura. The old homestead has not been the same since you left. As Father is hosting a soiree tomorrow evening, he has requested your presence."

She folded her arms across her chest. "Is this a directive from employer to employee?"

"On the contrary," Jeffrey said. "It is a chance for you to meet some of the more influential folks from the surrounding area. Most helpful should you need to raise funds for the school at some point in the future. You would, of course, be my partner for the evening. Father likes an evenly matched table. May I call for you at seven?"

Laura didn't hesitate long. Who knew what nuggets she might inadvertently glean pertaining to Hawkes's scheme for the Mason ranch.

"It would be my pleasure to partner you for the evening. Seven it is."

Amanda swooped on her the second the door closed. "You're going, then?"

"It would be rude not to," Laura said.

"What will you wear?"

"Oh, mercy." Laura rushed to her room at the back of the house. "I'd best pull out my gown and get it ready."

EVER SINCE THE night he'd been confronted by Hawkes in Yuma, Brody had taken to looking over his shoulder constantly, on the ranch and off. A fact which wasn't over-looked by his kin.

"You seem mighty jumpy these days," Braydon said, as they rode back to Bullet after doing business in Yuma.

Brody felt a twinge of guilt at not confiding in the others. "You never know what might be around the next corner."

He was still raw from that night, grateful that no one besides him knew the full extent of his hatred toward Hawkes. To hear Hawkes admit what he'd seen with his own eyes. That Hawkes was, in fact, the man who shot Brody's father dead.

He knew there was nothing to say one way or the other if his old man had cheated. Clearly Hawkes was as much of a poor loser then as he was now. Either way, Brody continued to patiently plan his strategy to enjoy every moment of taking Hawkes down. Once the time was right.

He patted his saddlebag, which contained the latest round of notes Hawkes had taken out against his ranch, which Brody had just purchased from the lender. Seemed his neighbor had been making some very bad investments of late, all of which played in Brody's favor.

"I've got a couple of things to take care of in Bullet," Brody said. "I'll meet you at the ranch."

Braydon shot him a look, but said nothing as they parted ways. Brody had a feeling his poker face might be letting him down where Laura was concerned. Which in no way stopped him from heading to the Cooke house where Laura was renting a room.

He wanted to see her. Not with any of the others at his side. Not caught off guard like that first day at the schoolhouse, or at the park when she'd spotted him following her. Surely, she hadn't been serious about fancying Jeffrey?

At the time he hadn't been able to see past his jealousy to think clearly. It was only later, when he was no longer distracted by her presence, that it occurred to him she might have concocted the entire story to keep some distance between them.

Perhaps he could invite her to join him for a little stroll in the cooler evening temperatures. He would find out how she was liking her teaching post. Maybe even learn the real reason she was here.

He was almost at the house when he was passed by a stylish carriage, complete with driver and team of matching black stallions. The rig smacked of Hawkes's borrowed money.

Brody hung back as the carriage pulled to a stop outside the very place he was headed. The carriage door swung open and out stepped Junior, dressed in his finery. Top hat, black coat and trousers pressed with a razor-sharp crease.

Brody watched in dismay as Hawkes Jr. bounded up the front steps. The door opened as if he was expected. From his vantage point he saw Laura appear on the other side of the doorway, her shimmering gown backlit by a lantern behind her. Enough light seeped out that he could see how her hair was arranged in a cascade of loose curls flowing over her shoulders, while she displayed what Brody considered an unnecessary amount of creamy bosom for a school teacher.

*Son of a—.*Brody clenched his fists as Hawkes took the shawl from Laura's hand and laid it over her shoulders before he took her arm and helped her down the steps and into the waiting carriage.

She'd been telling the truth, after all.

After a brief hesitation, Brody fell back a short distance behind the moving carriage. At first, he thought the rig and its passengers might be destined for a night on the town in Yuma. But as they reached Hawkes's lavish spread the carriage slowed and turned down the drive.

Looking toward the house, Brody saw an assortment of other fine carriages and rigs. Appeared old Hawkes was having a command performance that included Laura.

Realizing the futility of sitting out on the road stewing, he reluctantly turned his horse back toward Bullet and home. So much for his Saturday going-calling plan.

Not that the burning in his gut was jealousy. He was uneasy on several levels, knowing Laura was hobnobbing with Hawkes and his sort. It proved he was right not to trust her. Yet, no matter what had happened between them in the past, he didn't want to see her get hurt.

Ultimately everyone connected with Hawkes got hurt.

DURING THE FEW short days she had stayed at the ranch, Laura had never seen the ostentatious house all fancied-up for guests. The great hall, which ran the length of the front of the house, was alight with the glow of what looked like hundreds of candles.

Isabela's husband, dressed in a crisp white shirt and black trousers, greeted them at the door and took Laura's wrap. She felt the unwelcome pressure of Jeffrey's hand at the small of her back as he escorted her into the salon to join the dozen or so guests mingling and chatting, cocktails in hand.

Hawkes appeared at her side the second Jeffrey left to fetch her a drink. "So glad you were able to join us, Miss Kismet. I thought it was time you met some of the other townsfolk. It never hurts to know the right folk."

"Thank you for inviting me." Laura wondered if he was faking the friendly tone, or if he no longer cared that she had moved out from under his roof. Somehow, she doubted that to be the case. More likely she was here so he could keep an eye on her. She pasted on a tight smile. Two could play the game of cat-and-mouse.

Just then, an overblown young woman joined them and linked her arm through his, as if marking her territory. Hawkes gave the woman an indulgent look, the kind usually reserved for pets and small children. "This is Dolly. Dolly meet Miss Laura Kismet, the town's new schoolteacher."

"Pleasure." Dolly had an unpleasant nasally tone, which seemed to go along with her unnatural-looking bright auburn hair, long painted fingernails, and tight-fitting emerald green frock.

Jeffrey returned with Laura's drink, something cool and

tart, and proceeded to introduce her to the others, leaving Laura with her work cut out for her to remember names. Don and Estella Lucas would be easy to remember with their dark, Mexican coloring. Mr. and Mrs. Randall 'heavily into mining' Jeffrey whispered into her ear, were the most flamboyant couple. Dr. and Mrs. Parsons were the more elderly of the guests. Mrs. Parsons appeared to be hard-of-hearing, her head cocked to one side as she constantly asked the others to repeat themselves.

Laura was surprised to see the minister, Reverend Wesley, in attendance along with his wife. She wouldn't have expected the clergyman to be on Hawkes's guest list, unless perhaps her host was angling to stay on the good side of whomever was in charge of the afterlife.

The group was rounded out by Mr. and Mrs. Saunders. Laura knew Saunders to be the town's lawyer, whose office she passed each day on her way to and from the school. Jeffrey proved to be a master of small talk, leaving Laura the chance to nod and smile and sip her drink as she observed the others.

Hawkes must have some deep-seated motive for the gathering this evening. She only wished she knew what that motive was, and who the important players were.

Suddenly there was a commotion from the outer hallway. The loud voice of a newcomer was followed by the softer voice of Isabela. Hawkes jumped to his feet, as the newcomer blew into the salon.

"Sorry I'm late Hawkes. Folks." The tardy guest made what could only be considered a sweeping bow to those guests staring at him open-mouthed. The man was familiar, his accent foreign. English, Laura guessed, but he could have hailed from any number of British territories.

"Ladies and gentlemen, may I introduce our incoming guest, Sir Percival Bloom."

"Please, Hawkes. A simple Percy will do."

Laura narrowed her gaze. The reason Sir Percy looked familiar was because he'd been in the stagecoach with her and Jeffrey from Yuma to Bullet. She wished now she had paid more attention to the conversation between him and Jeffrey instead of staring out the window, lost in her memories.

To the best of her recollection, there had been no indicator at the time that the Englishman was acquainted with either member of the Hawkes family, senior or junior. Yet, suddenly, he appeared to be the guest of honor this evening.

She turned to Jeffrey. "Does your father conduct business at these soirees, or is it strictly social?"

Jeffrey smirked in an irritating way. "You know what they say. More deals are struck across the dinner table than all the offices in the USA."

"Do you believe that?"

"My father certainly does." Jeffrey lowered his voice for her ears alone. "He's working on a deal with Don Lucas. Some mining ventures between us and Mexico. Saunders will be handling all the details." His voice took on a boastful note. "And I'll be heavily involved, of course, in the day-to-day operations."

"I wonder where Sir Percy fits into that picture."

"Oh, not at all," Jeffrey said dismissively. "Percy is what some folks would call a 'treasure hunter'. He's after my father for funding for his latest venture."

"Treasure in Bullet," Laura mused. "Like buried treasure?"

"Nothing confirmed yet. But father does like a finger in every pie."

Over the buzz of chatter as Sir Percy introduced himself to each guest individually, Hawkes called for everyone's attention. "This way, folks. Isabela informs me supper is served."

Laura followed Jeffrey, who pulled out the chair on his right to seat her, while Saunders seated his wife on her other side. Mrs. Saunders gave her a dismissive glance, as if to say a schoolteacher was beneath her notice, and turned in the other direction to where her husband was deep in conversation with Don Lucas.

Laura found it interesting to note that Hawkes sat at the head of the table, with Sir Percy residing over the foot and the guests in between. If, indeed, she had been invited to 'round out the numbers' as Jeffrey had said, those numbers had just shifted with Sir Percy's arrival. Which made her wonder if there was a different reason for her presence.

The conversation between Percy and Saunders was cut short before she could hone in on it, as Hawkes once again took the floor. "Ladies and gentlemen, a toast. To acquaintances old and new."

Dutifully everyone raised a wine glass. A murmur of 'to acquaintances' rippled around the table before each of those gathered sipped from their glass. Don Lucas rose as Hawkes took his seat. Laura could tell from the look on Hawkes's face that he didn't like being one-upped at his own dinner table.

"Thank you for inviting us here, Señor Hawkes. I will be most interested to hear later of your plans for our partnership. And how you intend to remove certain obstacles from our pathway as we move into the future."

"Now, Don Lucas," Hawkes said. "We have a certain way of doing things here in Arizona. No business talk during the meal, just plain bad for the digestion. We menfolk will have our chin wag later over cigars and brandy. No point boring the little ladies with our discussion."

"Start with the small fork on the outside," Mrs. Saunders told Laura loudly as the first course was served.

Laura forced a smile. "Thank you, Mrs. Saunders. I'm no stranger to a formally set table."

"Well, la-di-da," her seat-mate sniffed.

The hard-of-hearing Mrs. Parsons leaned forward and spoke loudly. "I seem to recall, years back, a family in Yuma name of Kismet. Any relation?"

Laura kept her face impassive. She'd half-expected such a question might crop up during the evening. "I believe there were some distant cousins on my father's side some-where in Arizona. Is the family still nearby?"

"Oh, no." Mrs. Parsons chased a grilled sweetbread around on her plate. "Not for years now. How long ago was it they left, Arthur?"

"I'm not really sure, my dear."

Laura glanced toward the head of the table in time to see Hawkes's sharp gaze upon her, as if waiting for her reaction.

"Shame," he said, when she made no response. "It would be nice for you to have some kin hereabouts seeing to your well-being."

Laura made a face. "Not much solace when the kin are total strangers."

"Speaking of that," Dolly piped up, obviously happy to have something to contribute. "What do you all make of the Masons? Claim to be brothers, yet I hear there's no blood between 'em, to speak."

"There has to be some blood," said the reverend's wife. "Two of the brothers are the spitting image of each other. Identical twins for a certainty."

"Let me remind you we are all the Lord's creatures," said

Reverend Wesley. "Some men are brothers in their hearts with no blood tie. Others feel no tie with their kin at all."

"Blood has a way of showing the truth," Hawkes said. "And blood or not, the Masons are all bad news."

"Didn't you have a fellow by the name of Mason work for you some years back, Guy?" asked Dr. Parsons.

Hawkes made a sound between a snort and a grunt. "Not for long. Proved to be as lazy as the rest of the tribe."

"Seem to recall hearing he disappeared," said Saunders. "Ever find out what became of him?"

"Don't know and don't care." With that, Hawkes steered the conversation in the direction of the upcoming election. Laura wasn't surprised to hear him extol the virtues of the present sheriff who was up for re-election. So perhaps that's all this dinner was about. Some early campaigning.

Eventually the courses stopped coming, plates were cleared and the gentlemen excused themselves to the den, while the ladies retired to the parlor for coffee. Laura could barely contain herself. How she longed to be in the other room with the men.

She found herself next to Estella Lucas, whose English was excellent. "You must accompany your husband to the States a fair amount," Laura said.

"Si," said Estella. "There is talk, with the help of Señor Hawkes, we may one day make our home in Arizona."

"You must have family in Mexico. Won't you be sad to leave them behind?"

"We will travel back often," Estella said. "The mines know no borders."

"My husband says the exact same thing," piped up Mrs. Randall. "Quite a bit of talk these days about copper nearby."

"Copper?" Laura said. "I thought mining was all about gold and silver."

"Rumor has it copper is the new gold. Heavily in demand, and easier to get from the ground."

"Now, now ladies," yelled the doctor's wife. "Leave the business talk to the menfolk. Miss Dolly is set to tell us all about the new show she is in. I'm dying to see it."

Laura had no interest in hearing about Dolly's exploits on stage. Quietly excusing herself, she made her way to the kitchen to thank Isabela for her efforts tonight.

The housekeeper stood at the sink in front of a mountain of dishes, but instead of appearing happy to see her, Isabela's eyes widened in fear as they darted to what Laura knew to be a pantry on the far side of the room. Isabela clattered the pans and made an inordinate amount of noise. Seconds later her husband appeared from the pantry, red-faced.

Laura pushed past him and stepped into the pantry's dim interior. A crack of light showed through a tiny chink in the wall, which offered a perfect vantage point to see into the den. By pressing her ear to the wall, she could hear every word being said.

CHAPTER 6

Percy looked up as Laura re-entered the parlor. "There you are, Miss Kismet."

Laura nodded. She'd seen him take his leave from the den sometime earlier, once he'd made his pitch. Fortunately, he didn't ask her where she'd been.

"Hellish boring next door with the gents," Percy said to the room's occupants in general. "Plus, the smell of cigar smoke buggers up my nose...excuse my French, Ladies... something fierce."

"I expected the gentlemen would be discussing something of more interest to you than our polite ladies chat," Laura said.

"On the contrary," Percy said. "Miss Dolly has been regaling us with tales from back stage. Fascinating stuff. I'll never look at a play in London quite the same way again."

"Sir Percy has been on adventures all around the world," Dolly said in her irritating voice. "Makes me feel quite like a country bumpkin."

"Nonsense, my dear," Percy said. "You possess a most unique gift. The ability to entertain others."

As did Sir Percy, Laura thought, cynically. Witness the way he had the ladies hanging on his every word.

"What sort of treasure are you expecting to find here in Bullet?" the Dr.'s wife asked.

"That, I am afraid, must remain top-secret. Lest we be besieged with imitators," Percy said.

"Imitator treasure hunters?" Laura asked.

"Worse than that," Percy said. "The type of vermin who wait until all the difficult research and laboring has been done, then swoop in and claim the find as their own discovery. Most disquieting, really. Mum's the word, Ladies."

They all tittered. All except Laura.

"Do you really expect to find a treasure hidden near Bullet?" Estella asked in a bored tone. Perhaps Laura wasn't the only one who found Sir Percy tiresome.

Percy put a finger to his lip and made a shushing noise.

Dolly's laugh sounded more like a snort.

"Are you from London, originally?" Laura asked.

"Oxford actually," Percy said. "I was teaching about antiquities in the University there, until I got itchy feet to try my luck firsthand."

"How exciting," the reverend's wife gushed. "Like something from an adventure novel."

"I do declare," Dolly said. "You ought to write a play about your adventures. Maybe there will be a part in it for little-old-me."

"Perhaps I will one day, Miss Dolly. A starring role for our starlet here. Anyone else interested in taking to the stage?"

Laura wasn't sure why she didn't care for Sir Percy. There was just something a little too slick, a little too shiny and glib about the man for her liking.

Just then there was a loud rise and fall of voices in the

hallway outside the room. Laura smoothed her hair and hoped it looked as if she had never left the room. Before anyone could rise, the parlor door opened and the gentlemen trooped in, all except Hawkes. Laura angled her head around and glimpsed Hawkes in a heated conversation with a roughly-dressed man she had not seen before. The door closed before she got a good look.

On the other side of the room Jeffrey helped himself to a glass of scotch. Obviously not his first, judging by the way he was weaving slightly as he made his way toward her.

"One of Father's business associates," Jeffrey announced, his words slightly slurred. "Something has suddenly come up, and Father sends his apologies."

Jeffrey turned to Dolly. "Father has asked if you would be so kind as to entertain our guests with something on the pianoforte."

Percy clapped his hands. "Splendid idea."

Laura was far more interested in what was transpiring outside the room where Hawkes was, than inside. "Does your father expect to be long?" she asked Jeffrey.

Jeffrey shrugged and half-fell into an empty chair. But not even Dolly's playing could liven things up and soon those gathered began to rise with various murmured thanks and excuses.

As the guests mingled about the great hall and prepared to take their leave, Hawkes reappeared with a purposeful stride. "What's this about?" he roared to no one in particular. "The second my back is turned you scuttle off like a frightened bunch of rabbits."

"Not at all," said Percy smoothly. "Been a most interesting evening. Do thank you for including me at your table." The others murmured in agreement.

Percy turned to Dolly. "Miss Dolly, may I escort you

safely home?" He crooked an arm theatrically in the actress's direction.

Dolly responded with a curtsey.

Isabela's husband's eyes met Laura's, worry in his gaze. She tried to reassure him with a brief sideways inclination of her head that she wouldn't say a thing about his listening post, but wasn't sure he understood the message as he went to fetch the ladies' wraps.

Moments later, with the exception of Don and Estella Lucas who were overnight guests of Hawkes, the others left two by two, until only Laura and her two hosts remained.

Jeffrey weaved from side to side, eventually stumbling his way to a chair in the great hall. Chin hitting his chest, his eyes closed and within seconds he was snoring. Hawkes looked away in disgust.

"My son has yet to learn to hold his liquor."

"No matter. Your driver can see me home." She extended her hand. "Thank you for the most enlightening and entertaining evening."

"Not so fast." Rather than release her hand, Hawkes used his hold to pull her closer to him. "Jeffrey is not the only one who finds your company refreshing, Laura. Even if you did go against my dictates."

Laura raised her gaze to find his slitty, mean eyes on her, and in spite of herself a shudder went through her. This man was more than an enemy to Brody. He was evil. And genial as he might pretend to be, he was not a man who took kindly to being crossed, particularly by a lowly school teacher in his employ. She was saved by Isabela's husband who appeared with her light evening shawl.

Hawkes released her and snatched the garment from the man's hand. "I will escort Miss Kismet home." He inclined his head toward where Jeffrey slumped lower in the chair. "Leave him to sleep it off."

With that, he took Laura's arm in a proprietorial way and marched her out the front door to the waiting rig and driver, where he helped her in and seated himself far too close to be considered gentlemanly.

"It's really not necessary for you to accompany me home."

Hawkes's eyes took liberties with her person as he settled against the padded seatback. "What kind of host would I be if I left you to make your own way home? Town is full of ruffians and the such."

"I'm quite accustomed to taking care of myself," Laura said. "In Los Angeles—"

"I'm sure things were different in California. Here, we tend to be more old-fashioned. Do things the proper way. And like our women folk where we can keep an eye on them. For their own good, you understand. Also expect them to do as they're told and know their place."

Clearly, Laura had failed on all counts. She sensed an underlying threat in his tone, but refused to be cowed by it. Instead, she tried a different tact. "My father was a business man and I must confess such dealings have always fascinated me. A man like yourself must have many business interests in the area."

"Didn't get where I am by being stupid or lazy," Hawkes grunted.

"Did I overhear something about a partnership with the Mexican government? Something to do with copper?"

"I suggest you forget anything you think you might have overheard tonight. Keep your mind to your schoolhouse duties."

Laura refused to drop it. "Why was I invited tonight? Jeffrey said it was your idea. To round out the numbers."

"No, Laura. It was so we could have this little conversation. You crossed me once. Don't do it again or you'll live to regret it. No one crosses Hawkes."

Laura looked up, relieved to see they had pulled to a stop in front of the Cooke house. "I'll take that under advisement."

To her dismay, Hawkes alighted as well and insisted on accompanying her to the front door. She fished about in her reticule for the door key, which was heavy and had fallen to the bottom.

At last she had it in hand, just as Hawkes placed his hands on her shoulders and pulled her toward him. "I mean it, Laura. No one defies me." He ducked his head down as if he intended to kiss her. Laura started and straightened abruptly. The top of her head caught him under the chin, sending him reeling backwards.

His chin was hard. Her head throbbed from the blow, but he caught his balance and came back toward her. This time he grabbed her arms and held her hard. "Don't be forgetting. You work for me. You do as I say."

"Take your hands off me. I will not be ordered around by you or any other man. I quit! Find yourself another school teacher."

Hawkes let out a roar of a laugh. "It's not that easy, Miss Kismet." He emphasized her last name in such a way that she wondered if he knew who she was, then dismissed the idea as impossible. "You signed a contract."

"Contracts are made to be broken." Already she regretted her haste in signing the document. She had been so anxious to get the goods on Hawkes for Brody she had neglected her own interests.

"Not in these parts. There isn't a lawyer in Bullet or Yuma who will take your case. You show up at school on Monday or you'll find your comely ass in a jail cell faster than the proverbial bullet." He brayed in laughter at his own humor as he marched back to the waiting rig.

She was still shaking as the carriage drove away. She tried to unlock the door but her hand wouldn't stay still long enough for her to fit the key into the keyhole. Wretched man!

When she heard a footfall behind her, she opened her mouth to scream, only to feel a heavy hand clamped across her lips.

"Brody," she murmured against his palm. She'd know him anywhere, his touch, his scent.

"The same."

She caught the faint odor of whiskey on his breath as he took the key from her hand and inserted it into the lock. The door swung open noiselessly.

"Had to make sure you made it back safe. Never trust a Hawkes, father or son."

"That's a wise move," Laura said urgently. "Brody, I need to speak with you, but not here, not now."

"Can't say I trust you, either," Brody said. "Seeing how you work for the man."

"If you overheard anything tonight, you heard me try to quit."

"Why, Laura?" His voice was low, caressing, and so dearly familiar she wanted to throw herself into his arms the way she had when she was younger. Let him take care of everything. There was no family in the way this time. No reason they couldn't be together—

One look from him stopped the sentiment.

"Why what?" she said.

"Why did you come back? And don't bother trying to sell me on the notion of Jeffrey. I know you better than you think."

She lowered her gaze. She couldn't admit the truth. That she'd come back for him. That she'd never stopped loving him. That she hoped to atone for humiliating him all those years ago.

"I needed a job. I was homesick for Arizona. Take your pick."

In an unexpected move, he pulled off her bonnet and ran a lazy hand through her hair, snagging his big fingers in the freed strands. Laura stood, powerless to move. The years fell away.

He was so close his breath was warm on her skin. "Doesn't seem all that long ago that I picked you."

She gazed up at him and studied his dear, familiar face in the moonlight, all but holding her breath. So slowly it barely felt like he moved, he lowered his head toward her. When his lips found hers, her heart sang with joy. She was home. She was safe. She was with Brody.

She wrapped her arms around his neck and pulled him in closer, deeper, her mouth opening in welcome as his tongue teased her lips. Their bodies celebrated each other's rhythm as if they had never been apart.

He felt bigger than she remembered. More solid. Before, he'd been tall and well-proportioned, but gangly. Beneath her palms, she found arms and shoulders more heavily muscled; boy turned to man.

And what a man! Her limbs thrilled to the feel of him at every juncture they met and merged. Thighs, hips, chest.

Far too soon, they broke for air. She brought her hands up to clasp his face, to explore the square jaw, the angled cheekbones, the full lips she had once known so well.

"What happened tonight?" he asked. "You left with the son and returned with the father."

She stiffened, stepped back as if stung. Dropped her hands between them, clasping her fingers together to still the temptation to touch him more. To stifle the urge to reacquaint herself with every single inch of him. "You've been watching me. Having your brothers take turns. I suppose it was all your idea. Well, I don't like it one bit."

"Hawkes is bad news, Laura."

"I know that!"

"You don't know the half."

Laura glanced around, afraid someone might overhear them in the still night air. "We have to talk, but not here. I'll come out to the ranch tomorrow."

"Not the ranch." Brody spoke so quickly she wondered what he might be hiding.

"Where then?"

"Where we used to meet. Noon. I'll be waiting."

Laura nodded, half-afraid, half-hoping he might kiss her again. Disappointed when he didn't.

"Night, Laura." Two steps and he melted into the evening darkness as quietly as he had appeared.

She stared after him into the darkness with a half-smile. It was strangely comforting to know Brody had been there ready to leap to her defense if Hawkes had refused to take his hands off her.

"Do tell everything about last night," Amanda said, as she filled the kettle and put it on the wood stove.

Dutifully, Laura rattled off a list of everyone who had been at the dinner party.

"Not that," Amanda said. "Afterwards. Pretty sure I heard a man's voice. Did old Jeffrey get up his nerve to ask for a goodnight kiss?"

"Jeffrey was a little too far into his cups to see me home. I had to put up with Senior for that pleasure."

Amanda clapped a hand to her wide-open mouth. "And *he* tried to steal a kiss!"

"In a manner of speaking, I suppose. I wasn't having it. I tried to quit, but he's holding me to my contract."

"As you know, he doesn't take kindly to folks who try to cross him."

Laura nodded. "Threatened to toss my ass in jail."

Amanda's gaze was concerned. "You best be careful, Laura. He's a powerful enemy to have."

They ate and cleaned up from breakfast, during which Laura pondered her next move. In order to meet Brody, she required a horse or some sort of conveyance.

Later that morning she found herself at the livery arranging to hire a horse and a small carriage. She took the rig as far as she could toward the river before the road gave out, then tethered the horse in a patch of dappled shade near a sweet clump of grass before she continued on foot.

She heard the waterway before she saw it. Here, the desert-like conditions gradually gave way to a lusher land-scape with a variety of green grasses, the occasional splash of color signaling the presence of a few fading wildflowers. The path seemed a lot more overgrown than she recalled.

She hadn't gone far before she spotted Brody. Her heart gave a giant leap as she recalled the fervor of his kiss last night. The way he had felt trussed against her. Her limbs grew soft and pliable and she missed a step before she caught herself, careful not to appear too eager.

Instead, she took her time and drank in the sight of him.

Trousers from that blue jean material that was all the rage. A shirt that she would bet was one of his best. He hadn't shaved, which left his jaw darkened with the beginnings of an overnight beard.

His eyes, when he saw her, grew wary and she knew it was her fault. She'd hurt him so badly. Little did he know she'd hurt herself worse. Had cried herself to sleep countless nights as her heart bled for both of them. For the scant taste of happiness being ripped from their grasp.

"I wasn't sure you'd show up," he said.

"Of course, I would. I said so, didn't I?"

"People change. Ten years is a long time, Laura."

Funny, it didn't seem long. It could have been yesterday that she and Brody made their way here to meet, far away from the prying eyes of the townsfolk.

"True. Long enough for a lot to happen."

"Did your family find gold in Black Hills?"

Laura nodded. "Pa hit it lucky near the end of the boom. He knew enough not to stick around once he saw things begin to peter out."

"So you didn't stay in Dakota?"

She shook her head. "Ma passed away right about the same time Pa heard about a place out west called Los Angeles. City of Angels. Not much there at the time, but he got a tip that whole area was poised to really open up once the railway came west. He bought huge tracts of land for next to nothing. Almost overnight there was a big boom in real estate."

Brody said nothing, just continued to watch her.

She resisted the urge to fidget. Forced her hands to remain still, to stay away from the temptation of touching him. "What else do you want to know?"

"Is your old man still there?"

She shook her head. "He and Royston started to drink a lot. One night they never came home. Sheriff found them drowned in a water trough downtown. Figured they were drunk and thirsty." She shrugged. "I'll never know for sure what happened."

"You believe they just fell in? Both of them?"

"Doesn't matter. I saw no reason to stay. Already had my teacher's training. I heard about this job and here I am."

"You still haven't told me why you're here. You could have gone anyplace in the country."

She heaved a sigh. "That's true. I guess— I guess a part of me wanted to stop in and make sure you were okay."

Brody snorted. "Never heard yet of anyone dying from a broken heart. Have you?"

She could barely speak around the lump in her throat. She blinked back a sudden upsetting sheen of tears. "I know Pa hurt you that night. I'm so sorry."

"What he did to me was nothing compared to you, twisting the knife in my gut that day at the church."

"I know. And I'm sorry."

He brushed aside her apology as if it was a pesky gnat. "You said you wanted to talk to me. What about?"

She drew in a hasty breath. "I chanced to overhear a conversation last night at Hawkes's place."

His face hardened. Did he already regret kissing her last night? Agreeing to this meeting?

"Likely nothing I don't already know. Hawkes always was a greedy, controlling bastard, with his sights powerful set on owning every last parcel of land in these parts."

"There's more to it than that."

Her eyes implored Brody to trust her. To listen and to believe. Maybe together they could plan the next course of action.

Unexpectedly, he took her hand in his. Hope flared. He was at least willing to listen.

"I thought you might be more comfortable if we sat for a while."

For the first time she noticed the blanket Brody had spread in the shade of a Cottonwood tree. She clasped his hand between both of hers. "Like the old days."

The years fell away as he settled her onto the blanket and offered her a mason jar of sweet, cold tea. Her taste buds captured the memory. He'd fixed it just the way she liked it.

She took another sip, feeling the clash of flavors dance across her tongue. She smiled and held the jar toward him so they could share, the way they used to.

Her heart sped up as she watched the way he deliberately placed his lips in the exact same place hers had been. His eyes never left hers as he took a long drink, then passed the jar back to her. Her hand shook. Everything was identical to ten years previous, except nothing was the same. Life back then had been simple.

Unlike now.

Brody had trusted her then.

Would he ever trust her again?

"Two of Hawkes's guests were a married couple, high up in the Mexican government."

Brody nodded, appearing unimpressed. "Hawkes always has powerful people on his payroll."

"But the way he was bragging." She shuddered at the memory. "Assuring Don Lucas he would do whatever it takes to get his hands on your land. Poison the well. Starve you out. Pick you off one by one. Burn you out if he has to. Claimed he knew how to make it look like an accident. How no one in the town would miss a ragtag bunch of wanna-be ranchers anyway."

Brody leaned back on his elbows. "You didn't happen to overhear why he wants the land so bad, did you?"

Her heart in her throat, she nodded. "As a matter of fact, I did."

CHAPTER 7

Laura sat next to him, her deep blue skirt fanned modestly over her legs, nothing exposed except the toes of her boots. When she removed her bonnet and shook her hair free, she looked far more beautiful than Brody remembered.

The girl of his memories had matured into a confident, intelligent, caring woman. How had he ever let her go?

Then his head over-rode his heart. It had been her choice. Public humiliation and shame. His rejection witnessed by the entire town.

While she might seem sincere at the moment, he wouldn't put it past Hawkes to have sent her with some tall tale concocted to send him off on a wild goose chase. The fact that Hawkes wanted the Copper Moon ranchland dated back to his uncle's days and before.

"Funny. Hawkes talking about this in a way for you to overhear."

"It wasn't like that." She captured his hand and inspected it closely. Was she lost in memories of his hands caressing her bare skin? Because he was, and the memory caused an uncomfortable tightness in his britches.

She blinked up at him through lashes that were darker and thicker than he remembered. She wasn't wearing her spectacles today. For that matter, she hadn't been wearing them last night, either.

"I know what you're thinking. That Hawkes fed me misinformation in the hopes that I'd waste no time sharing it with you. I can assure you, he had no idea that I was listening."

She told him about the pantry, about pressing her ear to the wall. And everything she had overheard.

"He and Don Lucas are joining forces with a treasure hunter. They believe there is a sunken treasure ship buried on your ranch."

He snorted in disbelief. "Those old ghost ship tales? Sightings one day of a half-buried ship in the salt marsh, the next day only empty space. A ship filled with pirate plunder or Spanish gold, depending on the origins of the legend."

She shushed him. "In this instance the ship is supposedly filled with a fortune in black pearls. The company had a contract in the Baja, but a king tide pushed the ship up the river. When the tide receded, the ship was stuck in the salt marsh where, over the years, desert sand slowly buried the ship."

"On land that now forms part of the Copper Moon ranch?"

"Sir Percy was most convincing with his maps and his research."

"Such is the treasure hunter's way. They hoodwink their investors and abscond with the funds. Which is usually the only sort of treasure they're after."

He wasn't prepared for the twin dots of red that bloomed

in each of her cheeks. "I just wanted to share what I heard. In order for you would know exactly what it is that you're up against."

"Laura, don't think me ungrateful, but Hawkes has other reasons for wanting to get his hands on the ranch. Reasons that go back long before you or I were anywhere near these parts."

"I heard more after Sir Percy left. The others spoke at length of mining interests between Hawkes and the Mexican government. They didn't say where they intend to start mining. All I know is the pearl ship was the part that meant something because Sir Percy believes it's on your land."

He blanched, then smoothed over his expression, but not soon enough. He didn't like the way she was studying him. She knew him so well.

Once, he reminded himself. *No longer.*

Still, he didn't quite meet her gaze.

"Something about mining struck a chord with you," she said, her head tilted to one side. "What do you know about copper being the new gold?"

"I'm a rancher, Laura. I don't know squat about mining."

She wouldn't let it go. "What are you not telling me, Brody? What cards are you holding so close to your chest that I can't get even a glimpse?"

"Things you're better off not knowing," he said. "That way you can leave with a clear conscience."

She huffed out a breath. "Leave! Why do you think I'm even here in the first place?"

Brody was confused. "Because we arranged to meet where no one would see us?"

"Brody Mason, you are totally obtuse. Why do you think I came back to Bullet?"

His defenses rose. "I asked you that the other day. Got some cock-and-bull story that I didn't believe for a second."

"Oh for—" Laura flounced to her feet and stared down at him in a way that was foreign to him. Her chest rose and fell and her eyes snapped angrily. No longer a young woman desperate in love with him; he faced a Laura full-grown and in a temper such as he'd never seen.

He'd never really been around a woman spitting mad. His ma had always been quiet and sad. The church-ladies were meek and silent. The whores were, by turns, docile or eager to please.

Faced down by Laura, mad as a rattler, was a new experience. One he wasn't sure how to handle. Any time one of the brothers got royally pissed, Brody left them to stew in their own juices till eventually they came around like nothing happened.

Slowly he made his way to his feet, which felt better. More in control of the situation. "You came here because of the job."

She all but spat out her answer. "I manipulated Jeffrey into bringing me back to be the school teacher. Soon as I heard him babble about his father's plans for a ranch full of so-called brothers who were in the old man's way, I knew I had to come back here and find out what I could to help you. To learn what he was up to so I could warn you. Maybe even help you thwart him at his own game."

Brody reeled, as stunned as if she'd hit him across the face.

She'd come back for him!

Part of him wanted to grab her and hold her close; to never let her go. Another part of him, his wounded ego, wanted to reject her the way she'd once rejected him.

"Well, you've warned me and I appreciate it. Best you

pack up and be on your way before you get hurt in the cross-fire. If Hawkes finds out you were spying, you won't be safe anyplace near Bullet."

"I'm not leaving you again. I had no choice last time. This time I have a choice and I'm staying to see this one out."

"It's too dangerous."

She stamped her foot. "I'll take my chances."

"I won't allow it."

"I hate to tell you, Brody Mason, but you're not the master of me. I—"

Only one sure-fire way Brody knew to shut a woman up when she wasn't of a mind to listen. He kissed her. Hard and sure. A kiss designed to show her who was boss.

When he was done, she hauled off and fisted him one across the face. Must have put all her strength behind it, for she all but knocked him on his keister. He lurched back a step or two like a drunken dancer, one hand on his stinging jaw. He opened and closed his mouth a few times to make sure she hadn't broken something.

"What the hell, Laura!" he said, once he'd caught his breath.

Hands on hips, she snarled at him like a wildcat. "Don't you ever do that again."

"It was just a kiss."

"My ass it was!" She stepped forward right in his face, stabbing his chest for emphasis with each word. "You were trying to strong-arm me. To put me in my place. Well, let me tell you, this is my place, of my own choosing, and I like it just fine." She threw both her hands up between them, but at least she quit poking him. "Now quit being an idiot and let's figure out what all we're going to do about Hawkes."

Her words stung him to the core, either his pride or his

heart. He stiffened immediately. "Been managing just fine on my own since the day you left."

"Good. I expect you'll manage even better now that I'm here."

They faced off across the blanket, glaring at each other.

Brody backed down first. Rubbed his jaw with a rueful grin. Damn, she looked cute when she was mad. All puffed and righteous like a rooster with its feathers fluffed.

"If you ever get tired of teaching young'uns, you could get a job on the fight circuit. You pack quite a wallop."

A look of caring concern flashed over her face. She stepped close and took his face gently between her hands, turning his jaw toward the sunlight. "Shame what it takes to get you to listen."

"Heard you loud and clear, Girl."

That got her dander up like he meant it to. She flung her shoulders back, spine straight, head high. "I am not a girl!"

Her words reminded him of the first time they met.

"I know that, Laura." He caught her wrist, played with the cuff of her riding jacket, his thumb subtly grazing the soft skin of her under wrist. "We've both grown and changed. Going to take some getting used to."

Damn, her skin was soft. Softer than he remembered. He felt a tremor of want rip through him. She must have felt it too. Her breath caught. Her chest rose and fell as her breathing resumed. Different this time. Soft and airy breaths wafting over him as subtle as a spring breeze. As sweet as in his memories.

His dreams.

He cleared his throat. Time to take back control. "I've a mind we should head out to the ranch. Tell the others what you learned."

"What will they think about me being there?"

Brody cocked a grin she remembered only too well. "I guess they'll know that the best man won. And they can stop with the gifts and wooing."

"And if I was liking the wooing?"

He bit back what he wanted to say. How it was high time she learned how it felt to be wooed by the right Mason. "I guess that'll be up to you. I'll have to warn them not to get on the wrong side of your fist."

"Or my good nature."

Before she could say another word, Brody picked her up and swung her into the saddle, glad she was wearing her riding skirt. Seconds later, with the blanket tucked away, he settled behind her.

As he reached around her for the reins, his hands brushed the undersides of her breasts, not quite by accident. She was fuller than he remembered. His loins tightened as he recalled pulling the tight bud of her nipple into his mouth, feeling its sweetness dance along his tongue.

"My buggy is up near the road," she said, as if unaware of his body's reaction to their closeness.

His arms were snug around her waist. The top of her head rested just below his jaw. He inhaled the sweet fragrance of her hair, a sweetness that was essential Laura. A scent that had long haunted him in his dreams. He'd never expected to see her again, let alone hold her in his arms.

All too soon they reached the spot where she had left the buggy. He was loath to let her go.

He dismounted first and caught her against him as she slid from the saddle. To his amazement she didn't bolt from his arms, but leaned against him, melting into him, until their two bodies felt like one.

When she tilted up her face toward his, it felt as natural

as breathing to capture her mouth with his own, slow and gentle this time, giving her lots of opportunity to pull away.

She kissed him as though her life depended on it; as starved for him as he was for her. There was no awkward bumping of noses or clashing of teeth. Her mouth felt as if it had been created for him and him alone.

He ran his hands up and down the contours of her back, feeling the planes and angles of shoulder blades and ribs. Hands sliding lower, he smoothed the womanly indentation of her waist where it flared to the soft curve of her hips. His hands molded her closer to rediscover the way she fit against him; every curve, every contour.

When they finally broke apart he could barely breathe, as if she had stolen all the oxygen from his body. His muscles felt like jelly. Standing was difficult. She gazed up at him looking as bemused as he felt.

"You got better at that while I was gone," she said.

His hands rested on her shoulders, reluctant to let her go even for a second. "You bring out the best in me. You always did."

"I'm glad you remembered that part. Now let's go tell the others about Hawkes."

Because he couldn't bear to be further away from her than inches, Brody tied Phoenix to the back of her buggy, set her in, then climbed up next to her and took the reins. He drove with one hand, the other hand snugged against her waist, keeping her close.

HAWKES ENTERED the crowded café and made his way to the table in the far corner, scowling when he spotted Estella Lucas seated next to her husband. Far as he was concerned women had no place when men were discussing important business. "Lucas. Ma'am."

Lucas gave him a hard look when he didn't remove his hat. Too damn bad. He glanced around. "Don't know why we had to meet here. Instead of the ranch."

"I believe it's important we be seen as casual acquaintances," Don Lucas said. "We wouldn't want anyone in town to think we have something to hide."

"Course not," Hawkes said, aware of curious looks coming his way from the café patrons. Maybe Lucas had a point. Folks didn't often see him having a casual bite in town.

"Coffee, Mr. Hawkes?" The owner of the café, damned if he could recall her name, appeared at his side with a coffee pot in her hand.

"Obliged," he said, pushing his empty cup toward her.

"Pie's fresh made this morning," she added. "Can I tempt you with a piece?"

"It's very good," Don Lucas added, with a charming smile to the woman.

"Maybe later," Hawkes mumbled, staring at his coffee and wishing he had a healthy shot of whiskey to improve the taste. He settled for a generous measure of sugar.

"They really need a hotel here in town," Estella Lucas said. "I am growing weary of traveling back and forth from Yuma."

"No reason you couldn't have stayed back there," Hawkes said. "Never did have much truck with talking business when a woman's in the room."

Too late he heard a sharply-indrawn breath from Estella, punctuated by a cold look from her husband.

"Didn't mean no offense, Ma'am. Just that business

matters are kinda boring and difficult to understand for your fair sex."

"On the contrary," Estella said, coldly. "I take a great deal of interest in my husband's business dealings. All of them."

Don Lucas placed his hand comfortingly over that of his wife. "Indeed. Estella is what you might call, my good luck charm."

Hawkes grunted. Craziest thing he'd ever heard. Maybe he'd made a mistake partnering up with the greaser. Except he needed the man's financial backing.

"Money matters was always too much for my poor Ann to comprehend.

She was more than happy to leave all that man stuff to me."

"How fortunate for you," Don Lucas said, smoothly. "As I understand it was her money that helped you get established here in Bullet."

Hawkes bit back a hasty retort. Instead, he forced himself to give an affable laugh, which saw curious heads turned their way. "Got that all wrong. I'm a self-made man." He leaned forward and lowered his voice. "Miz Lucas, I take it you're fond of pearls? Especially the rare, black ones."

"I like pearls," she said. "I also happen to put great store in the role copper is about to play in our future. Ours and society in general."

BRODY AND LAURA arrived at the ranch amidst an unnatural silence, a notable lack of activity. Brody felt the hair rise on the back of his neck as they drove up to the ranch house. Everything was far too quiet. Far too still.

He leapt from the buggy and took the front steps two at a time, bursting into a totally empty ranch house.

Seconds later he returned in time to see Laura climbing down from her seat in the buggy, her face mirroring the concern he felt. "What's wrong, Brody?"

"Wait here." He didn't pause, but strode to the equally silent barn where only a few horses shuffled in their stalls.

"Anybody here?"

The horses stirred at the sound of his voice but no one answered. He blew out a breath. Something was up.

Back outside, he blinked in the sunlight as his eyes adjusted from the shade of the barn. For once, Laura had listened to him and stayed put. He untied Phoenix from the back of her rig.

"Brody, talk to me. What is it?"

"I don't know. Something feels wrong. A few of the boys might have gone into town, but no way they would all leave the ranch unattended. They know better."

He paused, torn. Part of him wanted to send Laura away, to pretend they'd never had this meeting. Shared a kiss.

He needed to get on with business. Running the ranch and methodically destroying Hawkes. Things he could accomplish far easier without worry about Laura added to the mix.

Then he remembered the way she shared what she had overheard. Information was power, especially when it came to the likes of Hawkes.

"Let's go for a ride. See if we can find out where everyone is."

At least he hadn't sent her away.

Laura knew him well enough to know that had been his

first instinct. So maybe she was regaining his trust somewhat.

Like earlier, he hoisted her onto Phoenix and swung up behind her. It was quite the sensation, the saddle horn snugged tight against her woman parts and Brody tucked up hard against her backside. She felt a definite tingling up and down her legs that came from more than just the motion of the horse.

When she felt Brody stirring behind her as if his breeches were suddenly too tight, she knew the feeling had to be mutual.

He cleared his throat as if having trouble breathing. "Hang on," he said, as he urged the horse from a walk to a canter and then into a gallop.

Hanging onto the saddle horn was all Laura could manage. Yet, despite the speed with which they covered the ground, she felt safe in Brody's arms.

Eventually Brody slowed their ride as they made their way up a crest of ranch land and reined to a stop at the top. Laura caught her breath. The land was lush and green due to some sort of irrigation system, beyond which the river wound lazily along the banks, sunlight dancing off its surface.

Which was not all that was dancing on the surface of the river.

Brody's brothers, all six of them, cavorted like youngsters as they ploughed waist-deep through the shallows.

"Bunch of school boys," Brody mumbled under his breath, as the men took turns dunking each other, pouring hats full of water overtop each other's heads, and generally splashing up a storm.

Brody guided Phoenix to the shore where the horse dipped his head and took a drink.

"Gentlemen," he yelled out, to get their attention. "In case you haven't noticed, we have a lady present. Keep yourselves decent."

Laura's eyes widened. Were the men naked?

Indeed yes.

Braydon, whom she remembered from that day in Yuma, was the first to step forward with a cocky grin, his hat strategically placed over his loins.

"Joining us, Brody? We figured it was a good day to bathe, to keep ourselves fresh-smelling in our pursuit of the lovely Laura Kismet."

Laura saw Brody's hands tighten on the reins in front of her, felt his arms cinch her even more closely around her middle. "Not that a bath isn't a good idea, but there will be no more pursuit of Miss Kismet."

"Oh, I don't know," Laura chimed in sweetly. "I was quite enjoying all the attention." She glanced over her shoulder in time to catch Brody's scowl. "Weren't you the one who implied you don't trust me?"

"Trust is earned, Laura."

She shimmied even closer. "Am I going about it the right way?"

She saw his mouth quirk as he tried to repress a smile, and felt his hold tighten possessively.

Straightening in the saddle, he addressed the bathers. "Family meeting at the house. Make yourselves decent."

CHAPTER 8

Brody turned down Laura's offer to help him with his horse and hers. Once Phoenix was brushed and fed, along with her gray, he led the way to the ranch house. Halfway there a streak of gray fur tore past them in a blur.

Laura stopped and pointed as the cat raced around the corner of the house. "Is that Smoky?"

Brody grunted. "Acts like she's still a kitten. Has to be on her ninth life at least." He clomped up the three front steps to the dusty porch, trying to see his humble home through her far-more-worldly eyes. The ranch house was time-worn, added onto over the years, serviceable and well-used.

He needn't have worried.

He opened the door and followed her inside, where her first response was a keen murmur of delight as she ran her hands over the scarred kitchen table that dominated the room.

She glanced up at him, her eyes brimming with excitement. "I remember when you told me you were making this."

He felt a muscle jump in his jaw.

She remembered!

"Turned out okay."

"Better than okay. It's beautiful." She glanced up at him, her head tilted fetchingly to one side. "And the stories I bet this table could tell."

He bit back a half-smile. "What happens on the ranch, stays on the ranch."

"No spilling secrets?" she asked mischievously.

Secrets.

Deliberately he changed the subject, turned from her. "Sorry the place is nothing fancy. Bachelor digs on a working ranch."

"Fancy is as fancy does," she said lightly.

He recalled her family home in Yuma. Most lavish house on the street. "You must have seen some might fancy places in your travels."

"Pa and Royston were never around much. Ma and I lived pretty simple before she died."

As before, he sensed there was a lot she wasn't telling him. "It's tough to be an orphan."

She placed her hand on his forearm, her touch light as a butterfly. "I know you understand because you've been through it. I don't talk about it to many people."

"Laura, I—"

His words were interrupted by a ruckus out front, which was just as well. He didn't want to fall back into the trap of him and Laura; of feeling like they were two halves of the same whole, each thinking and saying the same thing at the same time.

They both turned toward the open doorway. His brothers crowded in like a swarm of locusts, all six of them, with a stranger in their midst.

Bradley had hold of the man's collar and gave him a

shake as if he was a dog. "Found this guy skulking around out near the marsh. Some wild-ass story about searching for treasure. Offering to cut us in once he finds it."

Laura spoke up. "I thought you already had several business partners, Sir Percy."

The man's eyes lit up at the sight of a familiar face. "The lovely Miss Kismet. I implore you to tell these fine gentlemen that I am most sincere in my claim."

Braydon turned to her. "You know this joker?"

Laura nodded. "He and I were both guests at the Hawkes's ranch last evening."

"And now he's out here spying," Bradley said. "Doing Hawkes's dirty work."

"I'm sure he meant no harm," Laura said. "He probably didn't realize he was on private property."

Brody smoothly took back control. "Why don't you tell us, yourself, just what you were up to, Mister?"

The man brushed at his sleeves, as if smoothing away imaginary flecks of dirt or brushing away the memory of Bradley's none-too-gentle grip. "Sir Percival Bloom at your disposal gents. And the young lady is correct. I had no idea I had encroached onto private land."

Obviously relishing an audience, Sir Percy launched into a lengthy yarn about the ship of pearls believed to have got off course and ended up land-locked in the salt marshes before time played its hand and the boat eventually sunk and was buried.

Brody listened along with the others. It was close on what Laura had told him earlier.

Sir Percy continued his yarn, how he was convinced he had narrowed down the ship's last known coordinates, and using a scientific equation which meant nothing to anyone listening, had pinpointed its final resting place.

Brody met Laura's eyes across the room, before he cut Sir Percy off in mid-sentence.

"You spin an interesting tale, but as you can see, this is a working ranch and off limits to you or anyone else you might care to enlist in your cause."

"But—" Sir Percy seemed momentarily at a loss for words. "But you could be sitting on a fortune's worth of rare black pearls."

"Tell you what," Brody said. "Me and the others will have a little chat about this and get back to you."

Sir Percy looked deflated, but resigned. "I pray you, don't tarry long. I might be the first to arrive on scene, but I won't be the last." He glanced from man to man each in turn. "It's not just about the riches, you see. It's about discovering a little piece of history, outsmarting Mother Nature. Like a jigsaw puzzle if you will."

Brody showed him to the door. "One of us will be in touch."

"Here he comes," Hawkes said to his two cohorts, as they waited down the road from the Copper Moon.

"About time." His foreman turned toward Hawkes. "You really think Mr. Fancy Pants knows what he's talking about?"

"Doesn't matter one way or the other," Hawkes said. "Just so long as he sticks to the marsh and keeps the Masons distracted. And doesn't go poking around where he has no business." He raised his voice as Sir Percy came within earshot. "We were getting worried," he told Percy. "Just about ready to send in the cavalry."

"No cavalry required," Percy said, as he slowed his

mount near the men. "Despite what you said, those blokes seem like right decent chaps."

The foursome started off, Hawkes and Percy in the lead, followed by the other two. "Interesting terrain back there," Percy said to Hawkes. "Saw the opening to a cave up on the bluffs to the east that look like it might be worth exploring."

"Stay out of the cave," Hawkes said, more sharply than he intended. Catching himself, he clapped Percy on the shoulder. "I mean to say, you got your hands full once you get started in the sand flats. Me and Don Lucas are expecting you know what you're talking about, with them pearls."

"As I told you earlier," Percy said. "Treasure hunting is always a risky venture. Often times one comes away empty handed. Poorer but wiser."

Hawkes gave his head a shake. "Not this time, my friend. I got me a right good feeling about this." He shot Percy a look. "They give you permission to go poking around on the ranch?"

"Not yet," Percy said.

Hawkes coughed up some phlegm and spat it on the ground. "Told you it would be a waste of time to ask. Never you mind. There's always ways and means where those Masons are concerned. Matter of fact, I've got a nice little surprise for Brody Mason. Kind of a family reunion."

"I don't get it, Boss," said his foreman.

Hawkes turned to the other man. "You ever catch a fly when you were a kid? And pick off its wings? Just because you could?"

"Jeez, I dunno. Sounds kind of weird to me."

Hawkes shook his head. *Hired help!*

"Well, it's something similar I have in the works for

Brody Mason. A plan to cripple him, but not kill him. Not yet."

~

THE MASON BROTHERS, en masse, were a force to be reckoned with. The seven of them, shoulder to shoulder, dwarfed the generous-sized kitchen, and made Laura feel small and insignificant.

"Listen up, everyone." Brody, as eldest, was clearly the one the others looked to for guidance and direction. "Laura came to me earlier to tell me about this treasure hunter dude. He's somehow got linked in with Hawkes and— who was the other man, Laura? Some Mexican big-wig?"

"Don Carlos. Apparently, he and Hawkes are involved in other schemes as well. Mining and who knows what all else."

"If Hawkes believes there is any truth to this ghost ship fairy tale, he'll be redoubling his efforts to get his dirty paws on the ranch. Everyone be even more vigilant than usual out there. He's bound to strike when and where we least expect it."

One of the brothers, Laura still didn't quite have their names sorted, leaned against the sink, a toothpick in the corner of his mouth. "I assume you have a plan?"

It was obvious Brody had been giving the situation serious thought ever since he and Laura chatted earlier. "I say we give Sir Percy our blessing to come poke around as he chooses."

There was a babble of dissent. As the crescendo grew, each man trying to be heard over the others, Brody held up one hand for silence. Laura was impressed to see that one by one the brothers fell quiet, their respect for Brody obvious.

"You know what they say. Keep your friends close and your enemies closer. We're not sure which camp Bloom's in. More than likely his own. But he's not going away. Might as well let him have at it in plain sight where we can keep an eye on him."

"What about Hawkes?"

"Nothing's changed there." Brody glanced at Laura. "You happen to overhear anything last night that might forewarn us what he's planning next?"

She shook her head, feeling as if she had somehow let Brody down. *Again.* "He fancies himself a good guy. A gentleman. But he's got those mean, slitty eyes." She shuddered delicately.

"That big house and those fancy clothes don't make up for the fact that he's a—" The man speaking bit off his words at a warning look from Brody. "—he's a mean son-of-a-gun. Begging your pardon, Miss."

"What is Hawkes's background?" Laura asked. "Where did he come from? How did he get his start? I don't remember a lot from when I lived in Yuma, but shouldn't I have heard of him back then?"

One of the brothers took up the conversation. "Weren't nothing but a shack on the land back in the day. Him and the missus built that big fancy house. She was a lot younger than he was."

One of the others picked up the story. "Heard tell it was her money, too. Her pa and Hawkes had some sort of business dealings. Not sure what happened. Word was, her old man was killed. Guess she found a substitute father figure in Hawkes and married him so as not to be alone." The speaker sent a glance Laura's way. "Different times. More difficult to be a woman alone back then."

"Yes." Laura spoke more to herself than to the others.

"She'd have no rights to own land or handle her own money. She probably had little choice but to marry Hawkes."

"Saw the wife around Yuma a bit," Braydon said. "Quite a looker in her day, but always had this sad air about her."

One of the twins piped up. "Who could be happy married to that ornery old goat? They found her body in the pond out back of their big, fancy house. Took her own life, they said. But there's others hereabouts who think different. Think Hawkes did the deed. Rumor has it that Jeffrey isn't really Hawkes's son. That the old goat is sterile."

Brody broke in. "Those stories are all just speculation. Nobody knows for sure except Mrs. Hawkes and the poor soul isn't around to be telling any tales."

"Seems to happen a lot to people who get in Hawkes's way," Blake said darkly.

The brothers looked around the table at each other, nodding.

Laura spoke up. "Amanda Cooke said her mother has something over Hawkes. That Hawkes leaves the Cooke family alone because of what she knows. What if we were to learn what that something is?"

Brody gave her a bemused look. "Whatever Mrs. Cooke knows, won't do us any good. The lady has always managed to steer clear of Hawkes. It appears that we, along with this ranch, are plumb in the middle of his way."

Laura was incensed. "You can't just sit back and wait to see where and how he attacks next."

"It's not your problem, Laura. And being seen as friendly with us could prove dangerous." Brody glanced around the table. "The wooing of lovely Laura is officially over, boys. Laura, best you hightail it back to California. Forget you were ever here."

Laura opened and closed her mouth several times, but

no words came out. What could she say? That she intended to throw her lot in with Brody? To help him fight evil and emerge victorious? He'd laugh her right into next week.

"I need to finish the school term out," she said, finally. "After that, we'll see. If I can be of any help...." Her words trailed off. It was clear from the look on Brody's face that he had no need or want of her help. "What if, in the meantime, I befriend Sir Percy?" she said. "Take an interest in his research. Maybe find out something that way, based on his dealings with Hawkes."

Brody grunted. "Can't stop you from being friends with whomever you choose."

She cocked him a look. Dare she think he was perhaps the teeniest bit jealous? "Sir Percy arrived in Bullet on the same coach as I did."

"So?" Brody said gruffly.

"I don't believe Sir Percy was acquainted with Hawkes before he arrived in town. Jeffrey was the one who put the two of them together, saying how his father was the man to know around these parts."

"What's your point, Laura?"

"Things could have worked out very differently. All of you could have ended up partnered with Sir Percy instead of him and Hawkes."

"We don't have partners," one of the brothers said.

"Yeah," piped up one of the others. "Everyone we need, that we know we can trust or rely on, is right here in this room."

Laura nodded, well aware she was not included in that select group. But she wanted to be. Above all things, she longed to regain Brody's trust. And maybe along with it, the trust and respect of these men he called brothers. She envied their camaraderie, their obvious regard for each other, their close bond.

She swallowed a sudden thickness in her throat. She really was an orphan, all alone in this world. "Count yourselves luckier than most."

The silence in the room was almost deafening.

"I'm going to miss you all," she blurted out, in an attempt to break the silence. "I've never been wooed before."

Mentally she catalogued the lot of them. Bradley was the one who cared for the animals. Braydon was the ladies' man. Blake couldn't read, but was apparently brilliant with machinery. Barron seemed the more boisterous twin, Bishop the quieter of the two. As for Benjamin, she wasn't sure just what his claim to fame was. And she might never find out.

Several of the men guffawed. "Doesn't say much for Brody, does it?"

"Not now and not years ago, either."

Laura bit back a smile, happy to see the bantering was back.

"You staying for supper?" asked one of the twins.

"I, uh... No unfortunately. I'm expected back in town. But I'd love to some other time." She glanced over at Brody. "If it's okay with Brody, that is."

Brody subjected her to a silent, searching look. What was he thinking? That her motives were complicit? Did he wish she'd just go away?

"Good idea," he said at last. "It'll give this lot a chance to practice their table manners."

His remark was greeted by cheers and laughter. Soon after, the others scattered, muttering 'chores to see to', as they left, until it was just her and Brody alone in the ranch house kitchen.

Another awkward silence stretched between them.

Laura cleared her throat. "I'm not going away, Brody. You can ignore me all you want, believe whatever you want, but I fully intend to help in every way I can."

He continued to eye her with a measured gaze, not saying a word.

"I know you don't trust me or my motives. But I'm not leaving things this way between us. I aim to earn back your trust no matter what it takes. So there. You can quit trying your darnedest to chase me back to California. I'm here to stay."

Her heart beat so loud the blood was a rush of noise in her ears. She twisted her hands together.

Ask me to stay.

Tell me you want me to.

Tell me you're glad I'm here.

Tell me anything.

"Laura—"

She leaned toward him like a flower seeking the sun.

At that moment, whatever Brody started to say was interrupted by a loud knock followed by the door swinging open.

Bradley stood on the threshold. "Sorry to interrupt, Brody. Woman here asking for you. Claims she's your mother."

CHAPTER 9

B rody froze. "My mother's dead."

It had been years since he'd said the words out loud. He'd been reciting them to people since he was eight years old, and had been relieved to finally reach adulthood and have folks quit asking about her.

The woman standing behind Bradley stepped forward into the kitchen. Her unwashed dark hair had mostly come free from its scraggly braid and was liberally streaked with gray. Her clothing was tattered and soiled and appeared several sizes too large for her frame. Her face was lined from years of too much sun exposure, while her mouth curved downward as if a lifetime of disappointments had taken away her ability to smile.

"Brody." She half-opened her arms and took a hesitant step forward. Brody held his ground as if he was planted into the floorboards.

The woman before him bore no resemblance to his childhood memories of his mother with her bright smile and dancing eyes. In his last true memory of her, she had one finger pressed to her full red lips, swearing him to silence. Making him promise to keep her secrets.

He'd hated her for that.

Maybe if he'd blabbed, she wouldn't have run off and his pa wouldn't have been killed. How different his life could have been.

He searched her face, yet felt nothing.

Her voice was pleading. "Please say that you remember me."

He let out a weighted sigh. "Can't say as I do."

Silence stretched tautly between them. Brody was only vaguely aware of Bradley drifting back outside, leaving him alone with the two women who, together, had hurt him a lifetime's worth.

Her bony shoulders lifted in a sigh. "I guess that's to be expected, you being so young and all."

"I wasn't that young," Brody said, between gritted teeth. "I was old enough to know no decent mother runs off and leaves her husband and young son to fend for themselves."

"I did what I thought best," she said, eyes downcast. "It broke my heart that I couldn't take you with me."

"I bet it did." Brody turned his back, wishing that simple act would result in the woman's disappearance. Her presence churned up too many memories.

Too many old hurts.

"May I?" Without waiting for an invitation, she pulled out a chair and plopped herself at the table. "Don't suppose it's possible to get your old mother a cup of tea, is it?"

"I'll do it." Laura reached for the kettle on the back of the stove. A wisp of steam rose as she lifted it. Brody bit his lip to stop from telling her not to bother. She was just trying to help.

She looked at Brody. "Do you have tea?"

He pointed to a tin on the shelf over the sink.

"Unless you've got something stronger of course," said their unwelcome guest. "It's taken quite something to get here."

"Why did you?" Brody asked. "Come here."

She gave him a coquettish look. Did she even realize she was old and ugly?

"Thought I'd try out the new-fangled steam engine. Got me as far as Yuma. That's when I remembered your pa had a brother Dan lived out this way. Asked around and learned you had taken over the ranch. Folks in town was good enough to point me this direction."

She glanced up at him. "You grew up real handsome, son. And done well for yourself, I'm proud to see. Thank you, my dear," she said as Laura put a cup of tea in front of her, along with a jug of cream. "Is this your wife, Brody? Don't tell me I'm a grandmother." She faked a laugh. "I don't know that I'm ready for that kind of news."

"Neither," Brody said tightly. "I suggest you finish your tea and be on your way. Whatever you came here looking for doesn't exist."

"Can't a mother have a yen to reconnect with her only child? Her only relative left on this earth?" The woman made a big deal of blowing in her cup to cool the contents.

Brody spoke between gritted teeth. "If, and I do mean if, you are who you say, you gave up all rights of motherhood years ago."

She seemed unphased by his words. "I hear tell your pa was killed some years back. I always knew that nasty gambling habit would be the death of him."

"It wasn't gambling that killed him," Brody ground out. "It was his wife running off with another man that started him not caring what happened to him. That and a bullet from the gun of some poor loser." He didn't make mention that he knew exactly who that particular poor loser was.

"I didn't mean for anyone to get hurt, Brody. I just needed more than the life I had with him."

"The life you had with him and me, don't you mean?"

"I should be going, Brody." He started at the sound of Laura's voice; had clean forgot she was there. How much had he said in front of her? Too much, judging by the look on her face.

Laura was also smart enough to read between the lines of everything he wasn't saying.

"Do me a favor and take her with you."

The woman who claimed to be his mother straightened from her slump. "Now you see here, Brody. I am your mother. You'll not be putting me out like yesterday's trash."

He glanced at the clock near the stove. "There's a train leaves Yuma in a couple hours. I suggest you be on it." That said, he turned and stomped out the door and down the front stairs.

The woman looked coolly over at Laura. "Well, Sweetie, I guess it's up to you to soften him up as far as I'm concerned. 'Cause I have no intention of going any damn place."

Laura folded her arms over her chest. "When's Brody's birthday?"

"What?" The woman's brow furrowed into a straight line across her forehead.

"You heard me. Brody's birthday."

"Oh, that was so long ago I—"

"Even the worst excuse for a mother never forgets her own child's birthday. The day she brought him into the world."

"I don't like what you're implying, Missy."

"And I don't like what you're trying to do to Brody."

The unwelcome intruder slurped down the last of her tea and rose. "Tell you what. Whyncha give me a little tour while I'm here?"

"I'll do no such thing."

"Suit yourself. I'll just have a wander on my own then."

"You will not! You will march out there and wait while I get the horse and carriage. Then you will ride with me into Bullet, get yourself on the stagecoach to Yuma and out of Brody's life."

"Well aren't you just the protective little thing? I bet Brody likes that just fine. Every man's looking for a woman to take care of him, one way or t'other."

"Out. Now!" Laura pointed to the door.

Reluctantly, the older woman rose and shuffled out. Laura followed and closed the door firmly behind her.

"Wait here." She all but ran to the barn to collect her rented rig. The little gray was happily munching some oats that had been left for her by one of the brothers and didn't seem to appreciate being interrupted, as Laura harnessed her to the buggy and coaxed her out of the barn toward the ranch house.

She hoped to blazes that nasty woman wasn't Brody's real mother. She'd get her out of here, and... Drat, the woman was nowhere in sight. Since Laura hadn't passed her as she came out of the barn... Where could she have gone?

Laura let out an exasperated sigh. The one thing Brody had asked of her and she couldn't get even that right. What good was she in his life? Maybe he was right. Maybe she ought to go back to California.

She straightened, catching sight of the woman who claimed to be Brody's mother coming from the direction of the outhouse, and gave her a stern look as she ambled her way toward Laura.

Laura was keenly aware of the way the woman's head bobbed this way and that, checking out the surrounding ranch land, almost as if she was looking for something. Or someone.

"I told you to stay put."

The woman shrugged one bony shoulder. "When you gotta go, you gotta go."

"And now you really need to go," Laura said. "Off this ranch and away from Bullet."

Before Laura had the chance to climb into the carriage, Benjamin came riding up at a fast clip, signaling her to wait. He reined to a stop and dismounted, all in what appeared to be the same smooth movement.

"I'll see her into town, Laura. I think you should stick around."

"Stick around for what?"

He pulled her off to one side, out of earshot of her passenger. "For Brody," he said, low-voiced. "This one showing up out of the blue has really knocked him for a loop. Not that he'd let on for a second, but I know him. He's changed since you came on scene. And much as he might bark at you to get, it's opposite to what he means. He needs you. Even if he won't admit it."

Talk about knocked for a loop! Laura plopped herself down on the top step and watched Benjamin load that hateful woman onto the back of his horse, secretly glad she was no longer tasked with seeing the old biddy on her way, out of Bullet and back to wherever she came from.

Not for one second did she believe the woman was Brody's mother. Not when she couldn't even name his birthday. Let Benjamin be the one to send her packing!

Dare she even hope Brody needed her, the way Benjamin said?

Resolutely she stood, dusted off her hands, and clambered back into her buggy. Perhaps if she learned what Amanda's mother held over Hawkes it would be something Brody could use. Something to help keep all of them safe.

Halfway back to Bullet, she saw a horse and rider coming toward her. As they got closer, she recognized Benjamin and reined to a stop. He did likewise.

"What happened to that nasty woman?"

"Gave me the slip when we got near Hawkes's place."

"You're bleeding!" She saw a deep red puddle staining his shirt near his waist.

"Good thing she's a lousy shot," Benjamin said, between gritted teeth. He was pasty white and swaying in the saddle.

"Get in with me. I'll take you back to the ranch."

He dismounted with obvious difficulty and only managed to climb onto the seat with her help. Once seated he expelled a deep breath, leaned back and closed his eyes. Laura tied his mount to the back of her carriage, and for the second time that day made her way to the Copper Moon with a riderless horse in tow.

Since no one was in sight, she slipped her arm around Benjamin and half-carried, half-dragged him up the steps and inside, where he crumbled onto the settee.

She fetched a clean wiping towel and tore it into strips before she carefully peeled away his shirt from where the bullet had just winged his side. Thank goodness! She really wasn't in the mood to be digging around pulling out a chunk of lead.

She did her best to clean the afflicted area and apply her clumsy attempt at a bandage. He winced as she tied it tight, but she was happy to see the blood loss had slowed to a trickle.

"What happened?" she asked.

"Can't rightly say. All of a sudden I heard a shot so close my ears rang. Followed by a burning pain in my side, and she was gone. The horse bolted. I could barely hang on. She must have run into the brush before I could get turned around."

"I knew she was up to no good," Laura said, more to herself than to Benjamin. "What earthly reason would she have to show up claiming to be Brody's mother?"

"Never could understand women," Benjamin said. "No matter what their age."

"Sounds like you're a confirmed bachelor, just like the rest of them."

"I believe in keeping life simple."

"If that's the case, how did you manage to hook up with Brody and the others?"

Benjamin shrugged with difficulty and started to shiver. Delayed shock setting in, Laura surmised, and fetched a bed cover from one of the upstairs bedrooms.

She heard the clump of booted feet making their way up the front steps and turned around in time to see Brody fill the doorway. "What are you doing still here?"

"Don't worry, I'm on my way for real this time. Benjamin can fill you in. Once you patch him up, that is. That imposter pretending to be your mother shot him."

"What the—" Brody pushed past her to Benjamin's side. He didn't seem to notice as Laura left the ranch house.

Behind him, Brody was well aware the second Laura was gone. It was like the light had gone out in the room. In his life.

"Thought you were done with ladies shooting at you,

Ben," he said, as he unwound the makeshift bandage and inspected the wound.

"Could have been worse," Benjamin said between tight lips. Beads of sweat on his forehead showed talking to be an effort.

Once again Brody fetched the well-used first aid kit and a bottle of whiskey. Benjamin spotted the tweezers in his hand and grabbed the bottle, taking a healthy slug.

"She only winged me. No need to be poking around in there. "

"I see a few threads from your shirt. Sorry, Ben. This is going to smart some."

The rest of the troop arrived just as he had Benjamin cleaned up and into a clean shirt. Tersely he recounted what Benjamin had told him.

"Who is this crone?" Braydon said. "What game is she playing at?"

"Probably one more question for Hawkes. Where are you going?" he asked, as Braydon stood and strapped on a holster and gun.

"Junior has a habit of visiting the ladies on Sunday night. I'll pay the girls a visit myself and see what I can find out."

"I'll come with you." Barron stood also.

Brody nodded. "Bishop, you tag along. Keep these two out of trouble."

"Tough job, Brody," Bishop retorted, but he stood as well and strapped on his holster.

"Don't do anything stupid," Brody growled. "You're just three guys out blowing off some steam."

"The girls like the twins," Braydon said with a wink. "Twice the pleasure, twice the fun."

"Just keep your wits about you," Brody said.

As Benjamin napped where he sat, Bradley rose. "I'm going to go see to the animals." Which left Brody and Blake alone with the snoring Benjamin.

Blake looked at him for guidance, the way they all did. "What now?"

"Heck if I know," Brody said. "It would be easier to defend ourselves against a full-on attack rather than this slipping-through-the-shadows game of cat-and-mouse Hawkes seems intent on right now."

"Or is that just what he wants us to think?"

LAURA MADE her way back to the livery and from there to the Cooke house without incident. It had been quite the day! How on earth was she supposed to show up at the school tomorrow and pretend as if nothing had happened?

She found Amanda preparing the evening meal. How calm and orderly the other woman's life seemed. Laura cast an envious glance around the well-ordered home.

"There you are. I made extra in case," Amanda said. "I wasn't sure when you'd be back. Interesting day?"

To say the least, Laura thought as she set the table for the two of them. They had barely started their meal when she launched into what was top of mind with her. "Amanda, when is your mother due back?"

Amanda set down her fork and knife and gazed across the table at her. "I wish you hadn't asked me that."

"I need to know," Laura said earnestly. "There are things happening around here. Things I might need her help with. Information she needs to share, for everyone's sake."

"The Mason's sake, you mean."

"Not just the Masons. The entire town. The power Hawkes wields isn't right. Something needs to be done."

"It's been that way long as I can remember."

"Which in no way makes it right."

Amanda pushed her scarcely touched meal aside. "Ma isn't ever coming back."

Laura's mouth formed a round O of surprise. "Is she—"

"Oh, she's still alive. If you can call it that. She's in a sanitorium on the outskirts of Yuma. Just sits all day in a rocking chair, holding a knitted doll she made when I was young. Doesn't talk. Doesn't recognize me. Lots of days I wish she would just go to sleep and never wake up. There has to be something better in the afterlife than what she has here."

"I had no idea."

Amanda shook her head. "No one does. They think she's abroad. I don't know what would happen to me, or this house, if the truth came out. So I make sure it doesn't."

Laura rose and circled the table to kneel at her friend's side. "I am so sorry. It was sad when my own mother died, but at least I had closure. I could move on." As they hugged, she felt Amanda's tears dampen the front of her blouse. "That's an awful lot for you to be holding in."

"It's not just that. When the time was right, she was supposed to tell me what she has on Hawkes. To keep me safe as well. As long as Hawkes thinks she could show up any day, I should be fine. If he knows she's no longer able to expose him, no telling what he might take it into his head to do."

Laura sat back deflated. "What was your mother's mind like when she was—" She paused delicately. "The way she used to be?"

"Sharp as a tack," Amanda said with a sniff.

"In that case it seems likely she would have made sure

you would always be safe. In case something happened to her. Did she leave behind any papers? Any letters?"

"Whole bunch of stuff," Amanda said. "Including the deed to the house. Pa had it built for her when they were first married. I say he ran off, but Ma always insisted he was a victim of foul play." She sighed. "I never knew him; he disappeared before I was born, so we'll never know for sure. Ma left a stash of gold along with a fair bit of cash. I don't know where she got it. I'm real careful not to spend much. There was also an old newspaper article. About a gang of stage coach robbers. How they all disappeared after their last big heist."

"Weird thing for her to keep," Laura said. "Unless it has some significance. Do you still have it?"

Amanda nodded. "Afraid it's nearabouts crumbled to pieces after all these years. There was some jewelry, too. Stuff I never saw her wear."

LAURA COULD HARDLY WAIT to ring the dismissal bell the following day. As soon as the last student had straggled off, she locked up the school and headed for Yuma to the newspaper office.

Arizona city, as Yuma had been called twenty-five years earlier, had put out a paper once a week and the old, brittle copies were carefully archived to preserve the area's colorful history.

Laura was given a pair of white cotton gloves to wear, to protect the papers, but the fact that she was a school teacher helped convince the editor to let her access the archives.

The papers were catalogued into heavy black ledgers with the dates lettered on the covers. It took a while to find what she was looking for because she wasn't sure what year to start looking. After a few false starts, she finally found a string of stories on a gang of thieves targeting the stagecoaches heading west.

Gang members had never been captured, and the story speculated they had either been killed or drifted off to a different part of the territory to carry on their crime spree. According to witnesses, there were five of them, characterized by distinctive red bandanas which covered their faces. Over the years Red's Rowdies as they were known, had liberated untold amounts of gold, jewelry and cash from their victims. A veritable fortune.

Despite a huge reward on their heads and a number of extensive manhunts which led nowhere, the gang members always managed to stay one step ahead of the law.

She was so engrossed in her reading she didn't notice the new arrival in the room until he spoke.

"I always admire a woman with a sharp brain and an ability to do research."

"Sir Percy!" Laura knew she must look as guilty as if he'd caught her stealing apples from his personal tree. "Goodness," she said. "I thought I had the place to myself."

"I always like to learn some local color when I arrive in a new area. Before I start my treasure quest."

He stared intently at the page she had open, and she wondered if he could read upside down.

"That looks interesting. A gang of thieves and thugs in these parts who ultimately disappear with the loot, never to be seen again."

Laura forced a laugh and closed the ledger. "Likely more fiction than fact. You know these old stories get exaggerated over the years as they are told and retold. Hard to know what's real and what's embellished."

"I always find the stories are a lot more based in fact than one would expect."

There was a pause. "Fortuitous to meet you here," Percy said finally. "There is a small matter I hoped I might plead your assistance with."

She pulled off the special gloves she'd been wearing to handle the papers. "What might that be?"

"Access to the Copper Moon Ranch. It's an integral part of my plans and I can't move ahead without the blessing of Brody Mason."

"What makes you think I could be of any help in the matter?"

He gave her a look that probed far below the surface. "I have a feeling Brody listens to you, Laura." He pressed his lips together. "May I call you, Laura? I don't believe we got off on the best first foot together, you and I. I had no idea what sort of man Hawkes was when I first arrived."

"And now you do," she said. "Now what?"

"I have a much better understanding of certain—" He paused. "Situations in the area between the residents. I believe I'm in a position to be of some help to Mr. Mason. You see, Mr. Hawkes is under the impression he and I are closely aligned. When nothing could be further from the truth."

She crossed her arms over her chest. "What, exactly, would you like me to do?"

"I just want to meet with Brody. I'm confident I can be of some use to him in so far as what Hawkes is up to."

"And in exchange, he grants you access to the ranch for your treasure hunt?"

Percy's smile widened. "I knew you were clever as well as beautiful."

Laura's imagination ran rampant as she drove back to

Bullet. What if Hawkes had been a member of Red's Rowdies? That would explain where he got the money to buy the land the ranch sat on and build a big, fancy house. Except the money had come from Hawkes's wife, or so Jeffrey had told Laura. A wife who had mysteriously drowned in a pond on the property.

She returned her rig to the livery and was walking home enjoying the way dusk softened a landscape spiced with the aromatic smell of Cleveland Sage, when a man stepped out in front of her.

Brody.

"Laura, we need to talk."

CHAPTER 10

The husky timbre of Brody's voice reverberated through the soft evening air and teased the wispy tendrils of hair stuck to the back of her neck. Every nuance of her being leapt to attention with delight and anticipation. Or an attempt to shield her from more anguish.

She didn't know which. All she knew was that her awareness of him assaulted her on every level: sight, scent, sound. The hollowness inside her that had been a constant since that fateful day finally felt filled. Nerve endings quivered with anticipation. Wanting more. Wanting everything she could never have.

Including Brody.

She tried to spare them both further angst. "We have nothing to talk about, Brody. Not as long as you don't trust me."

"I want to trust you."

"There is no wanting. You either do or you don't."

He bowed his head, throwing his face into shadow. "That woman, who claimed to be my mother—"

"Is no more your mother than I am. The fact that she

shot Benjamin in order to get away..." Would the woman have shot Laura if she'd been the one taking her into town when she didn't want to go?

Brody must have known what she was thinking.

"I didn't mean to put you in any danger. I would never do that, Laura." He rocked back on his heels. "On some level I wanted her story to be true. Wanted my mother to come back. Wanted to hear her say she's sorry for leaving me the way she did."

"Don't lump me in with your mother, Brody. She obviously didn't care." Laura couldn't imagine leaving a child, no matter what the circumstances. "At least not enough. I cared too much."

"Cared so much you humiliated me in front of the entire town." His voice was bitter.

Her heart plummeted with a familiar ache. She knew she'd hurt him. Had known at the time he would likely never forgive her, yet she'd had no other choice. Her father would have killed him.

"Brody—"

He cut her off. "I thought I was over that powerful hurt. Inflicted by her. Compounded by you."

She glanced up and down the street, then heaved a heavy sigh. "You'd best come in." It seemed obvious he wasn't finished talking. And she didn't have it in her to send him away.

There were no lights on inside the house. She lit the lantern in the middle of the hall table. Its beam highlighted a hastily scrawled note from Amanda telling Laura she'd gone to see her mother and would be back tomorrow. Her heart rate accelerated. She and Brody were alone.

Brody moved about the room as if he'd been there dozens of times, lighting a second lamp. Then he turned to face her, the chiseled planes of his profile thrown into shadow and light. "I'm worried about you. About what you associating with me might mean where Hawkes is concerned. I know what that man is capable of."

She could only imagine how far Hawkes might go if provoked.

"I'm not about to live my life in fear. I just want to live every day." She moved closer to him. Tipped off his hat so she could see his face. Looked past the proud, strong man standing before her into his soul, the part he tried so hard to keep hidden. His wounds and his pain.

Aware she was largely responsible for those wounds and the pain they caused. Her hand trembled as she raised it to his face, traced the angle of his jaw, the fullness of his lips.

Was her love for him was enough to make him whole?

She'd never feel truly satisfied until she tried.

She tilted her face up to meet his gaze, took his hand and placed it on her bosom. She felt his hand tremble beneath hers, felt his hesitation in every corded muscle, every indrawn breath.

"Laura—?" It was a question, a benediction, a prayer. And the sweetest sound she had ever heard.

"Brody." Her answer was clear, her voice low but level in the dimly lit room.

She felt his surrender seconds before he drew her to him, caught tight against his length. When his mouth captured hers, it was firm and masterful, taking, controlling, melding her to him, branding her his.

For now, or forever, Laura didn't know or care. Right here, right now was what mattered as her mouth softened and soothed, tried to erase past hurts. Her hands moved over the strong muscles of his back, delighted by the effect her presence was having on him.

As was his closeness on her. Her limbs grew weak, pliable, her legs barely able to support her as she arched against him. They fit together so well, as if each of their bodies had been created with the other's in mind.

Somehow, they made it to the settee, where they tumbled together in a tangle of limbs, a melody of sighs and murmurs of pleasure.

Brody stretched above her, the fingers of his free hand linked through hers. His eyes watched her closely as if he feared she might change her mind. She tried to reassure him with her touch, her fingers tracing his features as if to commit them to memory.

He was so familiar.

So dear.

It felt as if nothing had changed between them, even though everything had changed. The years fell away. She was sixteen again, tucked up against Brody in their secret place, safe, she had thought, in their own little world. Until ugliness reared its head. And nothing was ever the same again.

She wiped her mind clear of past injustice. Focused instead on the joy of being with Brody, noticing and approving the changes the years had wrought. Her touch found him to be firmer, harder, broader than years ago. Exuding a mature confidence that was new to her.

A confidence she approved as he laid claim to her mouth again and whisked his tongue across her rosy lips before he smiled down at her, his hand still clasped to her bosom. "You've grown some."

She smiled shyly. "I hope you approve."

"Very much."

His tongue continued to tease her lips, coaxing them to part, to allow his tongue admittance. She waited, scarcely able to breathe. Afraid to move lest she ruin the perfection of the moment.

Of their own volition her lips opened beneath his, to be enveloped in an inferno as flames of need spread from him to her. She moaned softly as the blaze grew until her entire body felt on fire.

She felt sparks radiating between them, every juncture where his limbs brushed hers. She couldn't think. Couldn't breathe. Could only feel. Only want.

Wanting more.

She whimpered when, with seeming reluctance, he ended the kiss, although he continued to smile down at her as if pleased by her response.

She smiled back. "It appears someone has spent their time well these past years."

"Laura—"

She shushed him with a finger to his lips. "I have not had such tutoring as you. "But I'm most eager to have you teach me all that you have learned."

"*Laura.*"

It was a groan, a sigh, a murmur, a prayer. All of which she took for agreement. She leaned over and kissed him, deep and hard, mimicking his actions of moments earlier.

"Such an apt pupil," he murmured against her lips. "You sorely test my control."

"Good." She deepened the kiss as she nimbly unfastened the buttons fronting his shirt. Enough so she could place her palm against his skin.

With a hiss he ended the kiss, his moves reluctant as he insinuated a little space between them, and propped himself on one elbow to face her.

"We're not youngsters anymore, Laura. And I won't be

sneaking around with you. When, not if but when, the time is right—"

Suddenly there was a loud knocking at the front door.

Her startled glance flew to Brody, who was up and on his feet before she could open her mouth.

"Stay here."

She saw the flash of metal as he pulled his gun from its holster. Ignoring him, she scrambled from the settee and straightened her gown. She followed him to the open front door where he stood, gun holstered, speaking low-voiced to someone outside.

With one hand behind his back he waved her away, out of view.

He was protecting her reputation, Laura realized. For her hair was in disarray, her lips swollen from their kisses. It wouldn't take more than a glimpse for anyone to realize what had been going on between them a few minutes earlier.

"I'll be right there," Brody said to the visitor. Closing the door, he turned to face her.

"Who was it?" She all but flew into his arms where he held her for a moment, smoothed a hand through her hair.

And although he hadn't yet left, she felt the return of their old, familiar pattern. With it, came the pang of knowing he was on his way, leaving her with no idea when she might see him again.

"It's just the boys on their way back from Yuma. They saw my horse, and are anxious to share what they learned in the— in town," he finished.

"You're leaving." Laura pressed her lips together. It had always been that way, their time together furtive and secret.

She'd hoped this time might have been different. She'd

never fallen asleep in Brody's arms. And how she longed for that experience. Even once.

"We both know I can't stay."

He was right of course. Neighbors would talk if they saw his horse here all night, particularly should they learn Amanda was away.

She made a sad little bob with her head. Like earlier, he was focused on protecting her. So noble. If only his actions made her happy.

"We never did get that talk you came here for."

"I'll be in touch." He pressed a quick hard kiss to her lips, scooped up his hat and was gone, leaving her feeling more alone than she had ever felt in her entire life.

Outside, Braydon gave him a searching glance. "Hope we didn't interrupt anything important. Wanted to let you know right away what happened on the way to Yuma tonight."

"It's fine," Brody said, thinking to himself how fortuitous it was that they came by when they did. Being alone with Laura proved a temptation difficult to resist. But compromising her reputation was something he'd do everything in his power to avoid.

Things between them hadn't worked out ten years earlier. His life these days was a lot more complicated than it had been back then.

"What happened on the way to Yuma?" he asked.

"Found that woman in town," Bishop said. "The one who'd been out at the ranch earlier."

"Spitting mad and bitter," added Barron. "Seems Hawkes expected you to welcome her with open arms and take her in. Planned he'd have a spy in our midst."

"When it didn't work out, he dumped her on her bony ass," Braydon said.

"Where is she now?" Brody asked.

The men exchanged a glanced. "On a train west. Out of our lives forever."

"I hope you didn't pay her to get lost," Brody said. "If you did, she'll be back for more."

"Heck no. Fed her some drinks, hogtied her, threw her in the cattle car where she belongs," Barron said. "She'll wake up and won't have a clue where she is."

"Seems though," Bishop said, "next in line as Hawkes's spy is likely that treasure hunter fellow."

Brody digested what they had said. "Strikes me more like he's out for himself than to be anyone's puppet."

"Anyway, by the time we got to Madam Zara's, the girls were all busy with customers," Braydon said. "Only thing we learned is that Junior hasn't been around there for a while."

"Old man must have him on a really short leash," Barron added.

LAURA WAS RELIEVED to find Amanda there the following day when she got home from school. Her friend was bouncing around the way only Amanda could, jiggling from foot to foot as she waited for Laura to take off her bonnet and wash her hands.

"Leave that," Amanda said when Laura went to fill the kettle. "I have something you must see!"

Laura smiled indulgently as Amanda grabbed her hand and all but dragged her to the dining table. "Ma was having a good day yesterday. She even knew my name and talked about my pa. Then she gave me this. Had it tucked in her bible."

She smoothed out the heavily creased paper. Laura frowned. "It looks like a hand-drawn map."

"Exactly." Amanda beamed.

"Am I missing something?" The lead pencil scratches had faded over the years, and the paper yellowed so the drawing was difficult to decipher.

"See here." Amanda traced the lines with her finger. "This is the road from town. This is the river. And this is the Copper Moon ranch."

"Are you sure?" To Laura's eyes, the sketch could have depicted anywhere.

"Yup. See this dead tree here? It's like a marker near the gorge. And this, here." She outlined a different shaded part with her finger. "Looks like this could be the entrance to a cave."

To Laura's untutored eye, it was hard to tell how far away the area on the map was from either the ranch house or the irrigated pasture where Brody grazed and watered the herd.

"I've never been near that area of the ranch, but Brody would know exactly what the map shows."

"We can't tell Brody."

"What? Not tell Brody?"

"What if there's hidden treasure? Left there by Red's Rowdies before they disappeared."

"I don't follow."

Amanda let out a heavy sigh. "My pa rode with the rowdies. He promised ma he'd quit the gang once I was born. If there's loot hidden there, it belongs to me."

"Belongs to the original owners, don't you mean?"

Amanda's face fell. "I guess. Ma said she begged my pa not to go on that one last ride with the gang. Said she had a feeling something bad would happen." She sighed again. "Seems she was right."

"And you think maybe the gang members buried their loot way out on the Copper Moon before they lit out, never to be seen again."

"Ma is still convinced the gang was all killed. Said nothing else would have kept my pa away from her. From us."

Amanda moved to the bookshelves, pulled a book down and flipped it open. Laura saw the insides had been hollowed out, leaving just the edges of the pages, a perfect hiding spot. Out of the book's center her friend pulled a red bandana, brittle with age. "This is supposed to keep me safe."

"Is that what I think it is?"

Amanda nodded. From beneath the bandana she pulled an envelope. "You can read it if you want. It's a signed confession from my father, saying he rode with Red's Rowdies and naming Hawkes as the gang-leader."

"Does Hawkes know you have this?"

"He knows Ma has something left from my pa. Ma said he leaves us alone because he doesn't know for sure exactly what she has or how incriminating it might be."

"This is dangerous, Amanda. Hawkes is dangerous. I wouldn't put it past him to burn the place down, just to make sure whatever you have gets destroyed."

"Ma told him a long time ago it was in a safe at a lawyer's office in a different town."

"Why isn't it?"

Amanda shrugged, fingering the edges of the bandana. "This, and me, are all she has left of my father. I expect she couldn't bear to part with it."

Laura stopped at the café for her customary sweet roll the next morning, on the way to school. For a change, Georgina didn't greet her with her customary smile and quip. The woman, whose tired eyes and care-worn skin bore testimony to a hard life, was subdued and clearly distracted as she scooped up the sweet roll from underneath the glass-domed display tray and wrapped it up for her.

Laura started to pass her the payment, then paused before she handed it over. "Is everything okay, Georgina?" She knew how hard the woman worked from early morning to late evening in the café started by her parents when she was a youngster. Laura had seen the mother in the kitchen from time to time, clearly getting on in years, but still helping out as much as she could.

"Everything's fine." Georgina wiped her sleeve across her upper lip before she took the money, but her red-rimmed eyes belied what she said.

"You sure? Because if there's anything I can do."

Georgina gave her head a quick shake. "Nothing you or anyone else can do, Laura."

Unconvinced, Laura continued on her way. The classroom lessons she taught came automatically, while in the back of her mind she kept returning to her odd encounter this morning with Georgina. Something was definitely not right.

Which is why she locked up the school as soon as she had rung the final bell and the children had scampered out. Often she stayed late, but not today. Today she hot-footed it back to the café, hoping for a quiet word alone with Georgina.

She was in luck, for the café was empty, it being past the lunch hour and too early for the supper time crowd.

"Hello."

No response as she made her way through the unattended kitchen, which was even hotter than the front, thanks to the glowing oven and a pot of water boiling away.

The back door stood open, and she made her way toward it past empty wooden crates and shelves of canned goods. When she stepped outside, she spotted Georgina coming toward her from the direction of the outhouse.

The other woman's face was streaked with tears, which she dashed away with her apron when she spotted Laura. Her shoulders slumped, as if from the weight of the burden she carried.

"I knew this morning, something was wrong. Please tell me what I can do to help."

Georgina let go of a weighty sigh. "The sheriff came by the other day. Said there's been complaints, folks getting sick after eating here. Left a huge list of improvements that have to be made or he shuts me down."

"What sort of improvements?"

"Ventilation. New oven. The list goes on and on."

"Is this unusual?"

"There's been something every year. Always claims it's in the interest of public safety, but I usually manage to appease him one way or the other." Laura opted not to ask what 'the other' might be.

"But this year it's too much. I'll never manage to do what he says. I don't know what will become of me and Ma. This place has been our whole life. The customers are our family." She turned beseeching eyes on Laura. "It's all I know."

"Maybe Brody and the other Masons can help. They're fairly handy."

Georgina gave her head a stubborn shake. "I'm already beholden to Brody. If ever I can't pay my taxes, he helps me out. Hawkes and the Sheriff, they like to inflate the value and taxes so they can order a foreclosure. It's how Hawkes owns half this town, with his eye on the other half."

"What if you had an investor? A silent partner nobody knew about?"

Georgina gave a half-laugh, half-hiccup. "A miracle like that would take an angel."

"That's it," Laura said. "An angel investor. To lend you enough money to fix up the place and hire more help so you don't have to work so hard."

"Only people around here with any money are the menfolk. I got no ken with being indebted to a man. There's always other strings attached."

"Not this time," Laura said. "It's time the women banded together to make things happen. Good things for this town."

"I can tell you, Hawkes won't be liking that none."

"You leave Hawkes to me," Laura said with more confidence than she was feeling.

Neither of them noticed Hawkes's foreman, listening from around the corner of the building.

CHAPTER 11

At last Friday arrived in what felt like an unending week. Laura was beset by distractions that made it doubly hard to concentrate. Not only was she excited by her plan to secretly help Georgina, Brody was never far from her thoughts. She hadn't seen him since that night at Amanda's. What might have happened had they not been interrupted?

Each day, it seemed, the students grew more demanding, in line with the weather which felt unbearably stifling, even for Arizona. Tempers were frayed and fights among the students became more frequent, requiring all her patience and skill.

She was thankfully locking the door to the school when she heard the pounding hooves of a horse being ridden too hard and too fast. She turned to see Hawkes pull to a stop in a cloud of dust, his poor mount nearly frothing at the mouth as he sawed on the reins.

He dismounted and pulled an envelope from his pocket as strode toward her, spurs jangling overloud in the stillness of the afternoon. His slitty eyes raked over her, meaner than ever, and instinctively she drew back, but there was no place to go. The locked door was solid against her spine.

Laura fought for composure. "Mr. Hawkes. To what do I owe the pleasure?"

He thrust the envelope toward her. "Your last pay. Along with your letter of notice."

Laura stood her ground. Rather than extend her hand for the envelope, she left him holding it. "I'm afraid I don't understand."

"Couldn't be any plainer. Your services are no longer required." He tossed the envelope her way. She grabbed for it as it fluttered toward the ground.

"You're the one who told me I had a contract to honor."

"Consider it canceled."

"On what grounds?"

"On the grounds of you misleading us to get hired. Never would have brought you to Bullet had I known your past involved anyone named Mason."

Laura continued to eyeball him where he stood before her. More than once she'd wondered if he knew who she was yet pretended not to, for reasons of his own. He held out one stubby hand, palm up. "I'll be taking back the key."

"What of the students?"

"Not that it's any of your concern, but Miss Dolly's younger sister arrived in Yuma. She'll be taking your place."

"How convenient for everyone."

"Ain't no place in Bullet for folks causing trouble, asking questions, butting their nose in where it don't belong."

She'd known he was riled with her, even before the day she moved off his ranch and proved she wouldn't be pushed around. Luckily, he didn't know the half, or dismissing her would be the least of his actions.

"Suggest you head back to California and take up your

life back there." His words carried an arrogant sneer. "The Masons' days in Bullet are numbered, same like yours.

"I don't know," Laura pretended to choose her words. "Turns out I quite like it here. Already, I feel like I'm one of the townsfolk."

Hawkes all but growled. "You'll be heading out of town, and fast, if you know what's good for you."

"Why Mr. Hawkes, that sounds rather like a threat."

"You don't know who you're tangling with, Girlie."

Soulless eyes, Laura thought. *Eyes of a killer.*

"Consider yourself warned." Hawkes spun about, speaking over his shoulder as he approached his horse. "Bad things have a way of happening to folks to who don't take heed."

Message delivered, he remounted and took his leave.

Interesting development, Laura thought as she walked home. Threatened or not, nothing could have convinced her more to stay. And now that she didn't have to go to work every day, she had a lot more time to dig around for answers.

She toyed with the idea of heading out to the Copper Moon to find Brody. She could tell him everything she hadn't had a chance to the other night at Amanda's: what she'd discovered about Red's Rowdies, the map from Amanda's mother, and now Hawkes firing her. But she had a feeling he'd try and stop her from getting any closer to the answers. Men had a way of trying to protect womenfolk, even ones who didn't need or want protecting.

On the heels of her ruminations came a fresh flood of questions and regrets. Brody was her past. She'd come to Bullet seeking to make amends. Or so she told herself. Was she also seeking a way to make him her future? To start anew?

He'd made it clear that wouldn't work.

They had no future.

Best to finish up what she came here to do and move on. She had the means to make a new life any place she chose.

All around her, the café resounded with a hive of late afternoon activity. Laura sat quietly at a back table, pretending to be engrossed in her book and her tea. In truth, she was observing the flow of customers, looking for ideas to help Georgina expand the business.

She wasn't convinced Georgina had taken her seriously the other day when they spoke of an 'angel' investor, but Laura was determined to leave the folks of Bullet the better for her having been here, however short her stay.

She pulled out her sketching pad and started to rough out a few ideas for expanding the café. She noticed a lot of the patrons eating there had arrived on their own, and took up an entire table. And even though they knew some, if not all the other diners, and frequently paused to say good day, no one joined someone who was already seated. Instead, they chose an unoccupied table.

Laura watched, puzzled. She was new here, so couldn't pretend to understand. Was this a Bullet thing? Were the solo diners relishing a quiet time alone? Was each newcomer respecting the other's need for privacy? Or were they waiting to be invited? Afraid of being rebuffed?

She continued to watch and sketch. What if Georgina installed a bar running along the side of the restaurant in front of the kitchen, with stools at it? It worked for saloons. People wouldn't feel like they were intruding if they plunked themselves down next to someone they knew.

It should also be an easy task to open up the wall between the café and the kitchen, put in a pass-through. Food orders could be placed there and picked up, to be delivered far more efficiently than poor Georgina rushing in and out of the kitchen nonstop.

By the time Laura finished her tea and tucked her book and sketch pad back into her school satchel, she was quite excited. If only she had someone to share her thoughts with. Trouble was, she couldn't share her ideas without also divulging the fact that she was wealthy enough to make them happen. Folks hereabouts were bound to treat her differently if they learned she was an heiress.

On her way out she pushed open the door, only to have it jump from her hand to reveal Brody standing on the other side. They both froze, wordless.

Brody recovered first. "Hello, Laura." He held the door so she could make her way through, then let it fall closed behind her, so they stood face to face on the sidewalk.

He cleared his throat. This was not exactly how he fancied their first meeting since that evening at the Cooke house. He watched a faint tinge of color bloom in her cheeks. She tilted her head up in that forthright way he always admired.

"Busy week?" she asked coolly.

He took her arm and stepped to one side, out of the way of passers-by. "About the other night."

"Say no more," she said. "Your actions spoke volumes. Clearly you have had time to regret your impulsive behavior."

He let his hand fall between them, not daring touch her any longer lest he pull her into his arms. It was true when she first arrived his ego had welcomed the chance to reject her. To hurt her the way she had hurt him. But the more time they spent together, the less important that became until it faded from mind entirely.

They had so much that was good between them, it

scared him. He didn't feel right leading her on, making promises for a future that had no promise. He wasn't free to pursue her, to pursue anything past right here and right now. Not so long as Hawkes remained on the scene, itching to destroy his family and take ownership of the ranch.

"It's nothing you did or didn't do," he said gruffly.

"Well thank goodness for that. I'd hate to think that by throwing myself at you—"

"I didn't think of it that way."

"Well, you can relax. I'll be out of your life soon enough. Hawkes just dismissed me."

"What? Because of me?"

She gave her head a sad little shake. "Contrary to what you think, Brody, not everything is about you. Good day."

He watched her walk away, her back ramrod straight, knowing he should go after her, knowing that he couldn't. Knowing that letting her walk out of his life again was a huge mistake.

THE NEXT MORNING, bright and early, she eschewed her rented rig at the livery for a perky little chestnut named Patrice. They bonded instantly. "Are you up for an adventure?" she asked, as she stroked the mare's silky nose and fed her an apple. She swore those wise brown eyes understood, just from the way Patrice tossed her head, blew through her nose, and shifted from hoof to hoof as if impatient to let the adventure begin.

"We'll be back before dark," she called to the livery keeper, once she was mounted and ready to set off. Tucked carefully in the saddlebag was her reticule with the map she had pinched while Amanda slept, some bread and cheese, and a canteen of water.

The livery keeper raised two fingers to the brim of his battered hat in acknowledgement.

She'd spent considerable time studying the map in the early morning hours while the most of the town slept. She concluded Amanda had been right. The drawing depicted an area of the Copper Moon away from the ranch house, and no doubt difficult to access, but she had no intention of galloping down the driveway and past the house, alerting the brothers as to what she was up to.

Instead, she'd charted herself a different route into the far reaches of the ranch, to the spot near the cliffs where Amanda had pointed out what looked like the entrance to a cave. The alternate way would prove a trickier ride but she was convinced she and Patrice were up for it.

Hours later, she wasn't so certain. She also wasn't convinced she hadn't been riding in circles for the past several hours. The landscape in every direction was starting to look the same. The river, which she was using as her guide, didn't flow direct north to south, but meandered into tributaries and overflow canals, all of which looked far too familiar.

She gazed up at the sun, directly overhead and merciless in its burning heat, which her hat did little to shelter her from.

"Let's take a break," she told Patrice, as she dismounted near the bank of an overflow creek bed and a few clumps of grass for the horse to nibble on. Generally, this part of the ranch looked drier here away from the river, almost sandy. She remembered Sir Percy's mention of salt marshes and sand flats, with boats being buried by the sand once the river receded and the waterway dried up.

Of course! she thought. No wonder the map wasn't making sense. Over the years, the river must have altered its course dozens of times, depending on any number of factors. She was attempting to follow something drawn the way the land looked twenty-five years earlier.

How did Sir Percy manage, following clues from hundreds of years ago? His calculations had to be mostly speculation, not something she was any good at. She needed things in front of her clear and easy to follow, and this area of the Copper Moon was anything but.

Hah! Clear and easy to follow, like Brody. Could anything be less clear? Even their short exchange yesterday outside the café had been fraught with conflicting undertones.

After a short break, she was back atop Patrice, hoping she could find her way back. Or at least to the ranch house. She'd take the cold treatment from Brody over spending the night alone out here. Surely, if she followed the course of the river, it would eventually take her near familiar ground.

It was a good theory, just far from reality. As the day wore on, Laura became convinced that not only was she hopelessly lost, her wanderings were taking her further and further from anything familiar. She could be in Mexico for all she knew.

She recalled the childhood story of Hansel and Gretel leaving a trail of breadcrumbs to find their way back. When the breadcrumbs were eaten by the birds the pair had no idea which way was home. She hadn't even thought to try to leave any sort of a trail.

She dismounted, took out the pocket knife she had packed, and used it to etch an arrow onto the trunk of a spindly tree.

No one knew where she was. Would anyone miss her

when she didn't return Patrice to the livery? She swallowed her panic as the sun inched its way through the sky, taking with it the blazing midday heat. At least she knew which direction was west. For all the good it did.

She had been foolish to come out here alone. She was even starting to imagine things, like the sound of someone stealthily making their way in her direction. Or was it her imagination? Perhaps help was close at hand.

She sat down to wait, then shot to her feet when the image of a horse and rider appeared on the horizon, quietly coming toward her. As man and beast drew closer, she recognized Jeffrey.

"She's over here, Father."

Any relief she might have felt at being discovered dissipated at the sight of Hawkes, a menacing half-smile on his lips and an evil glint in his eye.

"Good job, Jeffrey. I'll take over from here. You head back. Take her nag with you."

Jeffrey's eyes met hers in a troubling glance. Laura had no doubt he would do whatever his father said. The way he always had.

"Jeffrey, please." She reached an imploring hand as he dismounted and came toward her on foot.

"You were warned. You should have listened." Jeffrey claimed the reins of Patrice, attached them to his own saddle, and turned back the way he had come.

BRODY FACED A SOMEWHAT HYSTERICAL AMANDA. The woman had shown up at the ranch blathering away about maps and secret caves and Laura, making absolutely no sense at all.

Hysterical women. Not exactly his forte. He sent Bradley a pleading look for help.

Bradley gave him an eyeroll. "Better go check on the animals," he announced.

Amanda grabbed Bradley's arm as he attempted to pass her. "Wait! Bradley. Please. You must listen to me. Both of you. Laura's in danger."

That caught Brody's attention. "What are you talking about? What danger?"

"I showed Laura a map my mother had from my father. I don't know exactly, but I have reason to believe it leads to something that could incriminate Hawkes. Laura was gone this morning when I got up. So was the map."

"I don't see how having your map would place Laura in danger," Brody said.

Amanda threw her hands in the air as if fed up with talking to totally obtuse human beings. "Hawkes. You know what he's like. If he gets wind of Laura poking her nose someplace he doesn't want it..."

Brody blew out a breath. "Surely she wouldn't—" He stopped himself midsentence.

Of course she would! Damn Laura and her unwavering desire to help in the war against Hawkes.

"Do you recall what's on the map?" he asked, forcing himself to speak slowly and patiently, when in truth he wanted to shake the story from Amanda.

Amanda waved one hand wildly, as if he had a clue where she was pointing. "The far reaches of the ranch. The map shows a dead tree. It appears to be some kind of a marker. Somewhere near the cliffs and the river gorge."

Brody exchanged a look with Bradley.

"If it's where I think you mean," Brody said. "That tree is no longer standing. Hasn't been for years."

Amanda's shoulders slumped. "If Laura can't find that tree she well could wander off in any direction and not be able to find her way back."

"Terrain can be tricky in spots if she tries to follow the river back," Bradley said.

Brody's anger over Laura's foolhardiness gave way to concern. It pained him to think of her, alone somewhere on an uncharted part of the ranch. An easy target for Hawkes.

"Does Hawkes know about the map?"

"I don't think so. He knew Ma had something over him, just wasn't sure what it was." Amanda's eyes grew shiny with unshed tears. "It'll be dark soon. There must be something we can do."

LAURA SWALLOWED any feelings of vulnerability as she stared up at Hawkes astride his big, black stallion.

Slowly he shook his head as he glared down at her. "Jeffrey's right. You should have listened. Smart girl would have packed her bags and lit from town when she had the chance. Guess you're not as smart as I gave you credit for."

"How did you find me?"

"Jeffrey might be a little slow in some regards, but when he spotted you leaving the livery this morning, he followed you. When it grew obvious where you were headed, he doubled back to alert me. Took us a while to track you, but weren't that hard. And here we are." The mildly-spoken words were at odds with the evil menace in his eyes.

"Where are we exactly?"

"Little too close to a spot I like to keep private."

"The cave?" Laura said.

He stiffened at her words. "Who said anything about a cave?"

Too late, she realized she should have kept her mouth shut. For all the good it would do her. It was plain Hawkes was not about to cart her safely back to town. Out here, he had any number of places to dispose of her body.

All she could do was play for time and hope for an opportunity to escape. "Everyone knows about the cave," she said glibly. "The children all talk about how their parents threaten to leave them there, should they misbehave."

His eyes narrowed till they were almost shut. "I don't believe you."

"Truly," she said. "Sir Percy and I were chatting about it just the other day. He thinks it may have some significance pertaining to the whereabouts of that sunken ship he's looking for. Puzzled me too," she added, as if they were having an everyday conversation. "I mean a ship's unlikely to have sunk inside a cave."

She watched him closely as she spoke. "Quite makes me wonder what it is about the cave. Perhaps something you want to stay hidden?"

She'd scored a direct hit. She could tell from the quick flash of emotion, the way his eyes widened, before his gaze once more narrowed.

He spat on the ground near her feet. "Don't matter what you think you know. You and me gonna take a little walk." With a grunt, he dismounted heavily, rifle in hand. "This way." He waved his rifle in the air between them. "Don't need more bodies to bury. I hear drowning isn't so bad. They say it's just like going to sleep."

Laura was desperate to keep distance between them, even as he forced her in the direction of the cliff where the river churned far below. For every step he took toward her, she took one back, never taking her eyes from Hawkes or his rifle.

"Is that what happened to your wife? She accidentally stumbled into the pond and fall asleep?"

"Ann's usefulness was long past. Easy enough to feed her a little arsenic, bit-by-bit, over time. Helped to make her more and more disoriented. Shame she lost her footing that night."

"I bet you helped her along."

As he backed her closer to the cliffs, the roar of the river grew louder. From her exploring earlier today, Laura knew the sheer rocky sides formed a steep gorge where the river narrowed and churned through before it widened out down river.

"Same thing happened to you, right there ahead. Lost your footing. Jeffrey saw you stumble but was too far away to save you. All he could do was return your horse, heart-broken by your fall. See, you two was courting. Came out here to get away from prying eyes."

Hawkes squinted. "Either that, or you were distraught when he rejected you and threw yourself off the cliff. Yup, that might make a more dramatic tale for the retelling. Townsfolk be devastated by the demise of their beloved teacher. Bet they talk about it for years to come."

"No one will believe Jeffrey and I were courting."

"They will. Boy can be a very compelling liar when he wants to. Plus, you were seen on his arm at a recent dinner party at the ranch. My servants and guests will back up the fact that you two were hot to trot."

Laura glanced from side to side, seeking a means of escape. If she cut and ran, she had no doubt Hawkes would simply shoot her in the back and dump her body in the river. Regardless of whether anyone believed his trumped-up story or not, he had the law firmly in his pocket. He'd got away with the murder of his wife, and no doubt countless others over the years. What was one more killing?

Hawkes kept nudging her toward the edge of the cliff until there was nowhere else to go. She looked over her shoulder to the water below, the calm surface belying the fact that the current was swift and deadly.

Think, Laura, think! She turned to face him, wondering if it was possible to grapple the rifle from his grasp. But he had another gun holstered on his hip. His free hand went to it, as if he was reading her mind.

"Who's the smart one now, Miss Laura Kismet? Thought you had Jeffrey so blinded by your 'poor little orphan' story that he took pity on you and offered you the teacher job. Truth is, I sent him to California to look you up and entice you here. He didn't know why, but he always does my bidding. Dependable that way."

He knew who she was all along!

"Why would you want me here?"

He cackled and looked inordinately pleased with himself. "You haven't figured it out yet?"

As he spoke, Laura wracked her brain. Anything to keep him talking. She was pretty sure he wouldn't shoot her point-blank. At least she hoped not. And the longer she stalled...

"All I know is you want Brody's ranch. Which has nothing to do with me."

He gave her that slit-eyed, tight-lipped smile she was coming to know meant he was not amused, but pleased about something altogether different.

"I figured you'd be the weak link in the chain to Brody, throw him off so he can't see nothing else. Worked pretty good. That boy's in such a lather, it'll be easy for my plan to succeed."

Laura's heart sank. By trying to help Brody, she'd played right into Hawkes's hand. She lifted her chin. "Wasted effort. I don't mean anything to him one way or the other."

"Doesn't matter now that your usefulness has come to an end. Almost a shame it had to end this way. I had originally planned to make it look like Brody killed you in a fit of jealous rage when he caught you with Jeffrey.

That would have got him out of my hair for a good long time." He gave an aggrieved sigh. "But you went and changed all that, poking around out here where you got no business. Hence, here we are. Doesn't matter which story I spin, the river will take care of the rest."

While he'd been talking, Laura had been studying her surroundings. No way she could make a run for it through the arid landscape. There was no cover. He'd gun her down.

Nothing at hand to use for a weapon.

There was only one thing for it.

She spun around and jumped.

CHAPTER 12

Hawkes peered over the cliff into the waters below, relaxing his finger against the trigger of his rifle with regret. He'd wanted to kill the bitch himself and dispose of her body. The result might be the same this way, but nowhere near as satisfying.

He was just re-mounting when he spotted a rider coming his way. He tensed, then relaxed when he recognized Bloom. "What are you doing out here?"

"You're not the only person who knows how to track," Bloom said mildly, not looking the least bit surprised to see him. "Where's Miss Kismet?"

"How the hell should I know?"

"I tracked her not far from here."

"That makes two of us. Guessing she vanished into thin air. Her and her horse." He laughed as if he'd just made an enormous joke.

Bloom wasn't laughing. "The trail back there gets really jumbled. I picked up a different horse and rider, leading hers with no rider. Know anything about that?"

"What are you now, the law?"

"Hardly," Bloom said. "Staying away from the law has become rather a priority of late. But Miss Kismet and I have united over our mutual love of history."

Hawkes studied the man. He didn't trust Bloom far as he could throw him. Didn't mean he wasn't willing to use him.

"Ain't no interesting history in these parts," he said. "Not until you find that ship you're after. You still believe it's someplace close by?"

"I do," Bloom said. "And unlike you, I have the owner's permission to be scouting out this part of the Mason ranch."

"Pretty soon I'll be the owner. A fact you'd be well advised to remember."

"You seem pretty confident," Percy said.

"Just mark my words and remember this little conversation," Hawkes said.

THE WATER WAS cold and hard as Laura hit feet first, sucked down into the black abyss. She'd gulped a huge lungful of air just before she went under and she held it as long as she could as she kicked her way back to the surface. After what felt like forever, lungs burning, she broke through, gasping for sweet, blessed air.

She sputtered and coughed as she treaded water. Her riding skirt and boots were a definite hinderance as she let the current carry her away from Hawkes. By the time she pushed her sodden hair out of her face to check out the cliff line he was out of sight. Good. Because the murdering bastard had no idea she could swim.

The current carried her some distance downstream to where the river widened and the waters slowed. Before long, she judged shore was within reach and had just struck out toward it when she saw a dark head pop up a short distance away. In blind panic she kicked in the opposite direction, only to hear what sounded like her name being gasped out. She turned back toward the other person in the water with her.

Brody! What the....?

She quickly swam to where he alternately bobbed and flailed, doing a great imitation of someone who did not know how to swim. Just before she reached him, he went under.

She swam just past where she lost sight of him, judging the darker shadow in the water to be him. She took a deep breath and dove down. Somehow, she managed to get underneath him and slowly propel them both to the surface.

He broke the surface flailing, his dead weight already starting to go under again, when she took a good swing and clocked him with her fist. He stopped fighting.

"Be still," she said. "I've got you."

She grasped him in her best rescue move, kicking the two of them slowly toward the shallow, sandy shoreline she recognized as being near the Copper Moon.

She saw several bodies pacing the shore. Brody's brothers. When they spotted her, two of them waded in chest high to grab Brody. She let him go in a wave of relief, too exhausted to take another stroke or step.

A third man scooped her up and carried her toward shore. She lay still in his arms, her limbs limp, concentrating on regaining her breath. He clambered from the water and set her on the ground alongside Brody, who lay unmoving on his back, eyes closed.

Laura struggled to sit up. "Roll him to his side."

Ready hands did her bidding. She had almost made it to

her feet when Brody stirred, coughed, and gasped for air. Thank goodness! She collapsed back down, the reality of what had nearly happened washing through her. They both could have drowned.

"Laura." He turned his head her way. Her name on his lips was a scratchy rasp.

"I'm here." She shuffled closer. "What were you thinking, coming after me when you can't swim?"

"Benjamin and I were circling around, trying to get to Hawkes without him seeing us. When I saw you go over—" He reached up and cradled the side of her face with one palm. "I couldn't bear to lose you a second time. And I figured, how hard could swimming be, really?"

He'd risked everything to save her!

Laura didn't say a word, just blinked back tears as she shifted until she was close enough to lay her head on his chest. She could hear the steady beat of his heart, the dearest sound in her life.

The brothers hovered around. "We best get you both back to the ranch house and into something dry." No sooner were the words spoken than one of the others showed up with a buckboard wagon.

Amanda rode next to the driver. She jumped out almost before the rig drew to a halt, and raced to Laura's side. "Thank goodness you're okay! I was so worried."

"Me too," Laura said. Looking around, she took in everything that could have been lost. Family. Friends. Future.

She turned to Amanda. "What are you doing here?"

"You were gone this morning, along with the map. I lit out here to tell Brody what I knew and where I thought you might have headed. I knew if anyone could find you and stop you from doing something foolish it was Brody."

"Thank you," Laura said, and meant it. Her throat was

stuck with things she wanted to say but couldn't. Chances were good she would have made it to shore on her own but to have a greeting committee such as this, friends who genuinely cared about her, Brody willing to risk all, she suddenly had no words.

In a house full of bachelors, the only dry garments they could find for Laura to wear were a pair of ridiculously baggy trousers from their younger years and a soft, well-worn chambray shirt that smelled comfortingly like Brody.

As she changed, grateful to be wearing something dry, she heard Amanda in the kitchen bustling about making tea and bossing the brothers. Laura gazed sadly at her riding boots, doubting they would ever be the same. She braided her wet hair to get it back out of the way, newly aware just how close she had come to being killed.

Everyone was jabbering away in the kitchen when she returned. Brody, too, wore dry clothing. Dark hair slicked back from his face revealed the dark shadow of unrest in his eyes.

"Hawkes has to be stopped!" he said, in a thunderous voice that halted all other conversations.

"I couldn't agree more." They all turned as one to stare in askance at the stranger who stood at the open front door, one hand lifted as if to knock.

Brody spoke first. "And just who might you be?"

"Ian Northrup. I have the grave misfortune of being Guy Hawkes's brother-in-law. It appears drowning is one of his favorite ways to dispose of people he wants rid of."

"Your sister—" Laura stopped.

"Made the bad decision to marry on the heels of our father's sudden death. Wouldn't put it past Hawkes if he didn't have a hand in that as well. By the time Ann realized what he was like, she was expecting Jeffrey. Hawkes had control of everything and she knew she couldn't possibly leave her son to that monster."

"And you had no idea she was so unhappy."

"I was in the north working my gold claim. We lost touch for a great many years. I was coming for her when I got word she had passed away. 'Accidentally drowned'." He shook his head. "All her life Ann was desperately afraid of water after a childhood incident. There is no way she would have gone anywhere near that pond."

Laura saw sadness shadow the man's eyes at the memory.

"Rather than rush in here half-cocked, I bided my time. Learned everything I could about Hawkes's dealings here. Not only did I discover there was no autopsy, I found out how chummy Hawkes is with the local authorities. When I heard you all were high on Hawkes's list of people in his way, I thought you might like to join forces against him."

Brody, as eldest, spoke for the seven of them. "What are you planning to do?"

"First, I'm getting Ann's body exhumed."

"You won't learn anything from that except she died from drowning."

"There might be something else," Laura said, remembering what Hawkes had told her out on the cliff before she jumped. "What if she was poisoned?" Nine pairs of inquiring eyes turned to her.

"Something Hawkes said when it was just the two of us out there. About feeding her arsenic, a little at a time. He bragged about it," she added.

"If you're right and that is the case," Ian Northrup said, "there will still be evidence of it in her remains."

"You still need to prove Hawkes was responsible," Brody said.

"First things first," Northrup said. "That man is not getting away with killing my sister."

Laura wrapped her still-icy hands around the warmth of her teacup and listened to the men making their plans, not surprised when they eschewed coffee in favor of something stronger.

Could this really work? Could they prove Hawkes had murdered his wife, attempted to murder her, and see him locked behind bars? Could the nightmare of Hawkes terrorizing the townsfolk in Bullet finally be over?

"I have a court order from Boston, where Ann was born, to have the body exhumed," Ian said. "If she was first poisoned with arsenic it will show up in her organs. After that, all we need is proof he administered the poison and pushed her into the pond."

"It's a tall order," Brody said. "Hawkes is known for covering his tracks. We witnessed him murder in cold blood and couldn't do one single thing about it."

Laura thought she heard him mutter 'yet' under his breath.

Clearly, someone close to Brody and the others had been murdered by Hawkes's hand. No wonder they hated him. She glanced over at Amanda, aware they were both thinking the same thing. That there were bound to be a lot more bodies discovered before this was over.

Eventually Ian Northrup took his leave, promising to keep the Masons in the know as far as the results of the autopsy on his sister's body went.

One of the twins, Laura was not quite sure which one, spoke up. "Maybe we ought to get back to what we were about before all this happened." She'd have to work on learning how to tell the two of them apart. She'd had Bishop pegged as the quieter of the two, but sometimes she wasn't sure.

"That's right," said the other twin. "We were about to celebrate old Bradley's birthday."

Amanda turned to Bradley and rested a hand on his forearm. "I didn't know today was your birthday."

Laura noticed her friend had done touched Bradley more than once already today.

Bradley flushed slightly. "It's not really."

Amanda frowned. "I don't understand."

"I was left on the church steps as an infant. No one knows exactly when I was born."

Laura was quick to see, not only the way Bradley shrugged it off as no big deal, but Amanda's reaction. As if she wanted to kiss Bradley's past hurts and make them go away.

Laura recognized the look because it was exactly how she felt toward Brody. If only she had the power to wipe away the past and make everything right between them.

"That's right," said Blake. "Every year we surprise him. Throw a birthday party when he least expects it."

"What a lovely idea." Laura glanced around the room from brother to brother. Even though they were kin in name only, it was clear they were closer than any blood could bring them.

"Are you sure we should be here?" Amanda asked, sweet dimples playing near the corners of her mouth, trying to look like the answer didn't matter. "I mean we don't want to intrude if it's family only."

"Heck," Bradley said. "It's a party. The more the merrier."

Brody nodded in her direction. "A happy end to the day's events."

Laura watched enviously as the brothers spilled outside, strung up lanterns, set out candles, and tended a calf being slow-roasted over a spit. Their camaraderie, the good-natured sparring, was something that had been sorely lacking in her own family. A couple of them brought out banjos and started with cowpoke tunes. Laura guessed they sang those tunes a lot when they were on the trail, driving the cattle to California.

Her clothes soon dried in the heat and it was nice to be back in her own things. She looked over at and Brody and wondered how he felt, here in the midst of the family he had carved out of nothing. His upbringing hadn't had the monetary advantages of hers, yet which of them now had the happier life?

Drinks were drunk, plates of food were consumed, the light faded, and still the party continued in full swing. Blake and Amanda were circling the yard, dancing. Laura couldn't help but notice what an attractive couple they made.

She glanced at Brody, who had stayed by her side pretty much the entire evening. Was he worried she still needed protecting? Was he sorry she was here? Were the two of them locked in the past with 'what if' regrets, or able to move forward into the future? He'd not said a thing since his one cryptical statement about not wanting to lose her a second time.

"Come walk with me," he finally said, as if sensing her unrest. He took her hand and pulled her to her feet. She followed without a word. As in the past with Brody, words never felt necessary. The connection between them had always been so strong.

This time, she'd prefer it if he told her exactly what was on his mind.

He led her away from the party, away from the lights and

merriment, to a slight rise that overlooked the ranch house in one direction and faced the river the other way.

The wind whispered through the sparse vegetation, adding its own special magic to the place and the company.

"Brody, I—" Even as she opened her mouth she had no idea what she might say.

"Ssssh." His fingers pressed against her lips.

She couldn't help herself. She parted her lips, drew his finger into her mouth and felt his sharp intake of breath before his mouth replaced his hand.

It was a long time before either of them spoke.

"I always figured this would be the spot I would build my own house. The house I would bring my bride back to."

Her eyes widened. He pulled her close. "I thought I lost you today. My fault because I was too stubborn and proud and had waited too long to tell you how I felt. That I want you more than just in my life. I want us to build a life together. Build a family and a future."

"Brody, I need to explain. About what happened. Why I did what I did."

He stopped her with a kiss. "That's in the past."

"There's more," she said. Even in the dim light she felt him tense, felt him start to withdraw, but she couldn't stop what she had started.

She reached for his hand, needing the physical connection. "I don't ever want there to be secrets or half-truths between us."

She felt his tension mounting, transmitted through his hand to hers, leaving her heart heavy. What secrets did Brody harbor that he didn't trust her enough to share? Hawkes? Or something else?

She cleared her throat and carried on. "You need to know my true situation."

Instantly she felt him relax. "That you're unemployed and penniless and in need of a husband to look after you?"

She gave him a teasing punch to the forearm. "I can look after myself just fine, thank you very much. And you as well, for that matter. Particularly if you're in water over your head."

He smiled down at her indulgently. "Then what?"

"I'm actually rather wealthy. An heiress in fact, thanks to Pa's real estate dealings before he died. And I have plans for that money. At least some of it. Starting right here in Bullet."

He didn't say anything, just stared down at the ground near his feet.

"It's a new world," she hastened to add. "Women no longer need turn their money over to their husbands."

Finally, he looked up and she saw he was biting his lip to keep from laughing. Eventually, he managed to pull a straight face.

"Do you love me, Laura?"

"Now and forever. More than life itself. Since the very first instant on that sidewalk when you sent me flying. I looked up at you and got hit by Cupid's arrow."

His smile widened. "So, you're not only beautiful and you love me. You come with the added complication of being wealthy."

"I was afraid my circumstances might.... I don't know." Put like that it sounded quite foolish. Even to her.

"I get it. You thought it might wound my pride to know you have more money than I do."

"Sometimes it works that way," she murmured.

"Not when two people love each other the way we do." He pressed a kiss to the top of her head. "I suppose this means you're hankering after a mansion like the one you grew up in."

"I want exactly what you want. A simple life, helping folk to better themselves." She waved an expansive hand to encompass the party going on behind them. "Everything you've created here, this home, this family, makes you the wealthiest man in the county." She could tell he was pleased by her answer.

"It'll take a while to get the house built. Can you wait till it's finished to be Mrs. Brody Mason?"

"I've waited ten years. A few more months shouldn't matter."

Secure in each other's arms, they barely heard the faint, drifting notes of banjo music, scarcely noticed the flickering lanterns in the yard. They were enraptured by the promise of their future together, the legacy they would build.

Brody held Laura as if he'd never let her go.

Much as he relished the thought of seeing Hawkes in jail where he belonged, in no way would it diminish the need for revenge that ran through his blood.

A few months later...

The sun shone brightly overhead, raining its golden sheen on the smiling faces of the 'dearly beloved gathered together on this day'.

Amanda clutched her bouquet tight to tamp down her excitement. She'd never been part of a wedding party before. Brody, the groom, stood next to his six brothers, all lined in a neat and serious row to his left.

Amanda could not rip her gaze from one particular brother, Bradley Mason. Ever since his birthday party when they danced the night away, her lovesick heart fluttered a little harder in his presence. Maybe today was the day he would realize how perfectly they were suited for each other.

The air stirred with a collective gasp as the bride appeared, truly radiant in a lace gown inlaid with hundreds of pearls, her eyes glowing with happiness and love behind her veil.

Amanda willed her nerves to settle down. There would be plenty of time after the ceremony to ensure Bradley was as dazzled by her as she was by him.

Thanks for reading *Brody's Bride*. You might not know how important reader reviews are, but they mean a lot. Just a short sentence saying you enjoyed the book goes a long way with new readers and puts a smile on this author's face.

Review wherever your purchased *Brody's Bride* or on Goodreads or BookBub.

And please keep in touch

Website: KathleenLawless.com
Facebook: facebook.com/kathleenlawlessnovels
Instagram: instagram.com/kathleenflawless
TikTok: tiktok.com/@kathleenflawless

If you haven't already done so, sign up for my VIP Reader's Newsletter and be the first to hear about free books, fan-priced sales, and my new series. http://eepurl.com/bVosbı

Keep reading for a preview of Seven Brides for Seven Brothers, book 2, *Bradley's Bride*.

Dear Reader

The American West in the last half of the nineteenth century offers my heroines a chance to assert their independence and also introduce them to a hero who is their match in every way. My characters have their own ideas of right and wrong, good versus evil, and deal with it on their terms. It wasn't called the Wild West for nothing. Life was about conquest, survival and persistence,

I love writing a historical genre where the reader, by the simple act of picking up the book, instantly suspends disbelief. She easily forgets about her world and her woes in a tale where no one needs to empty the dishwasher or take out the trash, and adventure lies around every corner.

As an author, it's fun to carry her away to a time and place where anything could, and often did, happen. The customs of the day and the manner of dress might be different from today's world, but people are still people. They laugh, love, hurt and heal. Celebrate and mourn. They live life large. And in the untamed wildness of the settling of the west anything can happen.

Read on for an excerpt from Book 2, *Bradley's Bride*.

BRADLEY'S BRIDE - EXCERPT
Copyright ©2019 Kathleen Lawless

Chapter One

What a picture-perfect day for a wedding! Amanda was so excited she could barely keep still next to her best friend, Laura, who was exchanging vows with Brody Mason. Laura looked truly radiant in a lace gown inlaid with hundreds of pearls, her eyes aglow with happiness and love behind her veil.

A beacon of happiness Amanda saw mirrored on the groom's face.

As she shifted her gaze from Brody to his six brothers, her eyes lingered on Bradley, third from the end.

The preacher's voice interrupted her perusal. "I now pronounce you man and wife. You may kiss the bride."

Laura turned and passed her the bouquet just before Brody gathered his bride close for the wedding kiss. Amanda sighed at the sheer romanticism of the day. As she sighed, her mind skipped back to that secret and joyful place. A magical evening here at the Copper Moon Ranch, and the dances she had shared with Bradley.

In typical male fashion, he had avoided her ever since.

Amanda watched the gracious way Laura flitted from guest to guest, thanking them for coming. A keg of beer had been tapped and its consumption among the gents added to the buzz of merriment floating through the air. A four-piece group of musicians began warming up on the make-shift stage and dance floor to the left of the barn.

Amanda circled the group of guests, wondering why she felt so lonely in the midst of a party. An only child, her life had always felt pretty solitary with only her and Ma. Living in a small town in the shadow of Yuma, Arizona, Amanda told herself she preferred the small-town life. But how could she be sure when that's all she knew? She felt restless. Ready for some sort of change. Harking back to the first day she met Laura.

On the far side of the dance floor she spotted Bradley standing alone, his face in shadow. Perhaps he felt as lonely as she did, part of the reverie but never really belonging. One more thing they had in common.

She was gathering her courage to approach him, suggest they share a dance like they had once before, when there was a loud clang of spoons against glassware, a signal for the newlywed couple to exchange a kiss, which was followed by whistles and catcalls.

As she looked around the happy gathering, she nearly missed seeing the back side of Bradley as he made his way toward the barn. Before she had a chance to talk herself out of it, she set down her glass and followed him.

She wasn't overly surprised by Bradley's destination. Somehow, she instinctively knew he preferred the company of animals over humans. As Bullet was too small to have a fulltime vet, Bradley often helped out nearby ranchers when they had an animal in distress.

The barn's interior was dim, its only illumination from the lanterns outside, the air peppered with the smell of hay and warm animal flesh. As she walked past the shadowy stalls and heard the occasional snuffle or stirring of sleeping animals, her feet made no noise against the straw-strewn floor.

She heard Bradley before she saw him. Caught the low murmur of his voice as he soothed an agitated mare in a nearby stall. She saw him crouch down and run a large, capable hand up the mare's front leg, as he spoke in soothing tones. Amanda stood still as stone, envying the bond between man and beast. The moment was both intimate and poignant.

Suddenly, aware she was intruding, she spun to leave but the hem of her gown caught on a nearby pitchfork and sent it clattering to the ground. Bradley bolted upright. Their gaze met.

"What are you doing here?"

Amanda opened and closed her mouth several times but couldn't seem to find any words.

She cleared her throat and tried again. "Maybe I was looking for you." She shocked herself with the boldness of her tone, along with the way she sashayed toward him as if she'd been doing it her entire life, taking her cue from the professional ladies she'd seen in town.

"Maybe I was remembering how well we moved together on the dance floor the night Laura was rescued. Wondering what else we might do well together."

Merciful heavens! Was that her speaking? She sounded like a total hussy. His eyes on her were dark, unfathomable, giving away nothing. Was he intrigued? Or repelled by her forwardness?

"I'm going to do us both a favor and forget what you just said."

When he made to brush past her, almost as if she didn't exist, Amanda couldn't help herself. "Bradley, I—" She reached for him, caught the sleeve of his formal linen shirt.

"Don't!"

One word.

Dismissive.

Final.

Before she had a chance to reply, their exchange was

interrupted by a ruckus outside. She started at the sound of shots being fired. They both dashed toward the door of the barn as more shots rang out.

~

Get your copy of *Bradley's Bride* today or keep reading to see more books by Kathleen.

ALSO BY KATHLEEN LAWLESS

Sweet Western Historical Romance

SEVEN BRIDES FOR SEVEN BROTHERS SERIES

Brody's Bride - Book 1

Bradley's Bride - Book 2

Braydon's Bride - Book 3

Blake's Bride - Book 4

Bishop's Bride - Book 5

Barron's Bride - Book 6

Benjamin's Bride - Book 7

Seven Brides for Seven Brothers Box Set 1 - Prequel & Books 1 to 3

Seven Brides for Seven Brothers Box Set 2 - Books 4 to 7

Sweet Western Historical Romance

WIDOWS OF THE WILD WEST

Hope

Janie

Sweet Western Historical Romance

MAIL ORDER BRIDES

Mail Order Olivia

Mail Order Rachel

Mail Order Martina

A Bride for Shane

A Bride for Riley

A Bride for Weston

Mail Order Noelle

Chelsea's Choice

Lila: Rescue Me Mail Order Brides

Here Come the Brides Volume 1

Here Come the Brides Volume 2

Sweet Contemporary Romance

Frannie (Always a Bridesmaid)

Baxter (Last Man Standing)

Blue Sky Island

One Cinderella Spring

One Stolen Summer

One Fantasy Fall

One Wondrous Winter

Sweet Christmas Romance Novellas

Holly's Wish

No Groom at the Inn

Steamy Contemporary Romance

SECRET SEDUCTIONS

Her Untamed Cowboy - Book 1

Her Undercover Cowboy - Book 2

Her Unwilling Cowboy - Book 3

Who Needs a Cowboy! - Book 4

Intimate Strangers

Steamy Historical Romance

Taboo

Unmasked

Reckless Rogues - Box Set of the 2 Books

Romantic Suspense

Final Heat

Afterburn

Women's Fiction

Fabulous at Fifty

For a complete book list visit KathleenLawless.com

To be the first to hear about Kathleen's new releases, special fan pricing sales, and also receive a free book, sign up for her VIP Reader Newsletter at http://eepurl.com/bVosb1

ABOUT THE AUTHOR

USA Today Bestselling Author, Kathleen Lawless, blames a misspent youth watching Rawhide, Maverick and Bonanza for her fascination with cowboys, which doesn't stop her from creating a wide variety of interests and occupations for her many alpha male heroes.

With nearly 50 published novels to her credit, she enjoys pushing the boundaries of traditional romance into historical romance, contemporary romance, romantic suspense and women's fiction.

She makes her home in the Pacific Northwest and loves to hear from her readers.

Sign up for Kathleen's VIP Reader Newsletter to receive updates, special giveaways and fan-priced offers. http:// eepurl.com/bVosb1

KathleenLawless.com
Goodreads | BookBub
Facebook | Instagram | TikTok